'You were ver
quietly.

With his North A
pliment sounded
Hollywood movie. Alanna told him so, wanting to lighten the shock.

'If I were John Wayne,' he said, 'the next move would go something like this. . .' Slowly he moved his hand from her shoulder to the back of her head, twining his fingers in her hair. She found herself holding her breath, waiting. . .

Dear Reader

We travel the world this month, and introduce a new author to our list in Rebecca Lang, whose MIDNIGHT SUN takes us to the far north of Canada. We think you'll like her! Margaret Barker is back with THE DOCTOR'S DAUGHTER, a rewarding change of pace and style. Then to Australia for Judith Ansell's HEARTS OUT OF TIME, and Marion Lennox's ONE CARING HEART, both tear-jerkers you will love! Excellent holiday reading.

The Editor

!!!STOP PRESS!!! If you enjoy reading these medical books, have you ever thought of writing one? We are always looking for new writers for LOVE ON CALL, and want to hear from you. Send for the guidelines, and start writing!

Rebecca Lang trained to be a State Registered Nurse in Kent, England, where she was born. Her main focus of interest became operating theatre work, and she gained extensive experience in all types of surgery on both sides of the Atlantic. Now living in Toronto, Canada, she is married to a Canadian pathologist, and has three children. When not writing, Rebecca enjoys gardening, reading, theatre, exploring new places and anything to do with the study of people.

MIDNIGHT SUN

BY
REBECCA LANG

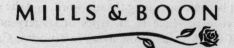

MILLS & BOON LIMITED
ETON HOUSE, 18–24 PARADISE ROAD
RICHMOND, SURREY, TW9 1SR

*First published in Great Britain 1994
by Mills & Boon Limited*

© Rebecca Lang 1994

*Australian copyright 1994   Philippine copyright 1994
This edition 1994*

ISBN 0 263 78707 9

*Set in 10 on 11½ pt Linotron Times
03-9407-57329*

*Typeset in Great Britain by Centracet, Cambridge
Made and printed in Great Britain*

CHAPTER ONE

'THIS is the final call for passengers on First Nation Air, flight 821, to Yellowknife, Northwest Territories. Now boarding at gate six.'

The young woman at the refreshment counter in the departure lounge waited for the announcement to be repeated in French before drinking the last mouthful of her coffee and throwing the styrofoam cup into the nearest waste-bin. The sudden increased sensation of excitement, tinged with a certain apprehension, made her wonder momentarily whether she had been wise to consume two cups of the very good coffee before taking off into the unknown.

She had deliberately waited until the final call, not wanting to sit long on the aircraft before take-off, or to join the early rush of passengers. Not that there had been much of a rush. It looked as though there would be at least a few empty seats on the flight to the city of Yellowknife in Northern Canada, her immediate destination. People were rather thin on the ground altogether in this departure lounge of Edmonton Airport, Alberta, that dealt with domestic flights.

Lifting up her two bulging in-flight bags, she made her way towards gate six. A seat had been specially reserved for her from the start of her journey in Toronto, since she was something of a VIP, so she had been assured by the personnel at the Toronto headquarters of the Northern Medical Development Corps, for whom she now worked and who had sent her on her way. They had said it to boost her ego, she suspected.

5

Up until now the whole scene had taken on the feeling of a dream. The churning excitement in her stomach told her that this was for real, now there was no turning back. This was not even the last leg of her journey. From Yellowknife there would be yet another trip to the remote northern community of Chalmers Bay, on the Arctic Ocean, where she was to work for the next six months.

'Boarding card, please, miss.' She fumbled to get the boarding card from the side-pocket of her handbag, juggling her coat, bags, a book and a magazine.

'OK, miss. Straight ahead.' The check-in clerk handed back her portion of the boarding card.

'Thanks.' This was it! Her legs felt wobbly as she negotiated the last few yards of the covered gangway to the opened aircraft door. Fumes from the engine filled her nostrils.

Three weeks ago she had been in Birmingham, coming to the end of a job contract at a hospital there, wondering where her next place of employment would be, because the post that she had applied for in Canada had not yet been offered to her, even though she had been short-listed for the job. From then on everything had happened very quickly. It had been one mad rush to get her papers in order and to make travel plans, so that now she felt in a permanent state of breathlessness.

'Welcome to First Nation Air.' Two smiling flight attendants waited to direct her to her seat. 'Row 21, seat H, miss.'

'Thank you.'

Making her way slowly along the narrow aisle, she did not notice the man who watched her progress with interest, appraising her with a practised eye, until she was almost upon him as she peered at the row numbers on the overhead luggage bins. The aircraft was considerably smaller than the one that had brought her from Toronto to Edmonton the day before, certainly smaller than the one that had brought her across the Atlantic just over a week ago. She found herself wondering what sort of craft would be taking her on the final leg of her journey.

There were only two seats in the window section, one of which appeared to be hers in Row 21, the one next to the aisle. The other seat was occupied by a man whose long legs seemed barely able to fit into the confined space. She looked down from her scrutiny of the row numbers and met his eyes. His were grey, intelligent and shrewd, with an alert expression of unmistakable interest. So this was to be her travelling companion.

'Excuse me, please.' Another late-comer made to squeeze past her in the narrow aisle, causing her to drop her magazine and book almost in the lap of the seated man.

'I'm sorry.' She bent forward to retrieve the book and at the same time her shoulder-bag slipped down her arm to fall with a clunk on the empty seat.

The stranger smiled, picking up her things with hands that looked strong, sensitive and capable, as well as tanned. Indeed, his face was also incredibly tanned for early May, she noted with a passing surprise. Here was a man who had obviously not spent the last few weeks in the frozen North, even if that was where he was going. He seemed to unfold himself with a casual ease as he stood up.

'Allow me.' Taking the heavier of her two bags from her, he stowed it in the bin above their heads, followed by her coat.

'Thank you.' She was beginning to feel a little flustered and gauche, aware that she was the outsider in unfamiliar territory beside this very attractive stranger who, with his slight North American accent and casually smart clothing, was obviously very much at home.

When he returned to his seat she was able to subside gratefully into hers, glad to be relieved of the bags. As a special dispensation she had been allowed to take extra baggage, which she was going to need for a six-month stay, during which she would need bulky clothing for the unpredictable weather of the Arctic and the cold that would come after the very short summer. When she was finally settled, the man beside her turned to her again.

'Excuse me for asking.' He had a pleasing, low drawl. 'Are you sure you're in the right seat? I believe this seat was reserved for a colleague of mine. We're supposed to be travelling together.'

For the first time she looked at him properly, noting his clean-cut features, the straight nose, the chiselled mouth, the firm square jaw. He had crisp dark hair, cut fairly short. A classically attractive man, she thought, almost too attractive—redeemed from being yet another Hollywood movie type by the obvious intelligence in his grey eyes, a certain perspicacity that made her feel sure it would be difficult for anyone to hide anything from him. What a curious thought!

'Er. . . I'm fairly sure I'm in the right seat.' She consulted again the crumpled boarding card. 'Yes, here it is.' She passed the card over to him. His scrutiny confirmed that the seat was hers.

'That's odd,' the man said, looking at her somewhat more curiously than he had before. 'I was expecting to meet up with a Dr Hargrove — Alan Hargrove. I sure hope he's on the plane.'

'That's me,' she said in surprise. 'I'm Dr Hargrove — Alanna Hargrove.'

'What? No kidding!' His elegant jaw dropped visibly.

'There must be a mistake. I wasn't told anything about a woman.'

'Who are you?' she asked bluntly.

The 'ding-dong' of the intercom interrupted his reply. 'Good morning, ladies and gentlemen,' a hearty voice boomed out over the sound of the engines, the Canadian accent very pronounced, 'this is your captain speaking. Welcome aboard First Nation Air, flight 821, to Yellowknife. Our flight will take approximately two hours and twenty minutes, arriving in Yellowknife at 1300 hours. The temperature in Yellowknife is four degrees Celsius, clear and sunny. Now please fasten your seatbelts and prepare for take-off. We wish to remind you that there is no smoking on the flight. Thank you. Have a nice day.' The captain's voice clicked off, to be replaced by soft music as the engines revved to a high-pitched roar.

Her companion said nothing more until the aircraft had stopped climbing and there was a welcome aroma of coffee wafting forward from the aft section, with the clatter of the refreshment trolley being wheeled out from the galley. Then he cleared his throat before speaking again.

'So you're Dr Hargrove. . .working with the Northern Medical Development Corps?'

'Yes, I am.'

'Going on to Chalmers Bay?'

'Yes. You must be Dr Dan McCormick. I was told that you might be on this flight.'

'No, I'm not Dan.' There was a rueful note in his voice. 'There seems to have been a monumental screw-up somewhere. You were expecting Dan and I certainly wasn't expecting a woman. Dan McCormick had an accident, broke a leg skiing out west in the Rockies. He'll be out of commission for a while. I was asked to replace him at very short notice, hence the screw-up, I guess. I can't say I was thrilled by the request; I've just spent the winter up at Chalmers — not an experience I'd want to wish on anybody — and was just recuperating in Barbados. I hadn't anticipated going back just yet.'

'Oh, I see,' she said politely, experiencing a creeping fear that things were starting to go wrong before she had even got to her destination, which did not seem like a good omen. She would be damned if she would show any of her apprehension to him, especially since he thought of her presence as a screw-up. The NMDC had told her quite a lot about Dan McCormick, especially that he knew a lot about life in the North and would have been able and willing to teach her. Now she had to start again from square one with this total stranger who was clearly disgruntled that he now had a female colleague.

'As far as I'm concerned, there's no mix-up,' she said. 'I've known for over three weeks that I would be coming here. When did Dr McCormick have the accident?'

'Two days ago. I got calls from him and from the NMDC in Toronto asking me to come back right away. They couldn't find anyone else at such short notice. They staff the place at Chalmers with people who do a six-month rotation maximum. That's about as long as anyone can take at a stretch.'

'So I understand,' she murmured. 'I suppose I wasn't informed about the accident because I had already left Toronto for Edmonton by the time they knew about it.'

The refreshment trolley rattled to a halt beside them. Alanna welcomed the interruption, not looking at her companion as he accepted coffee. Being on good terms with one's only medical colleague was absolutely essential in such an isolated place as Chalmers Bay. Common sense dictated that much, and the fact had been repeatedly stressed to her during the brief, intense orientation period that she had recently undergone in Toronto at the NMDC headquarters after her rather hasty arrival from England where she had been recruited. Survival in remote places depended so much on mutual co-operation. This man seemed to be overlooking that good advice.

'Let me introduce myself,' he resumed, making an obvious effort, it seemed to her, to recall a charm of manner that usually came naturally to him. 'I'm Dr Owen Bentall. We seem destined to be colleagues at Chalmers Bay. . .unless something can be done about it.' That sounded ominous again, cancelling out any charm he had managed to dredge up.

Automatically Alanna took the hand that he held out to her, feeling her heart give a jump of alarmed recognition and her features become empty of expression. 'How do you do?' she said formally, hoping that the shock she felt was not apparent.

So this was Owen Bentall! Her brother, Tim, had told her about him. As well as the name, she remembered epithets her brother had used to describe him. . . merciless. . .arrogant. . .cold. Tim should know. . .yet she did not think he was cold, at least not with women, in spite of his remarks. Even in her shock she was able to think that, coolly. Yes. . .he could be merciless at times, no doubt. Her intuition was seldom wrong. How ironic that fate should have given her Owen Bentall. . . when she had expected Dan McCormick. And how odd. She began to wonder whether he knew who she was. She had to be so careful.

'What did Dan McCormick think about you?' he asked. 'About having to work at such close quarters with a woman?'

'I've no idea. I don't know whether he was consulted. Does it matter?'

'You think not?'

'I mean, this is the 1990s. . . I understood that men accepted women these days as colleagues.'

'Perhaps you don't understand the living arrangements where we're heading, just how closely we'll have to accommodate ourselves to each other. . .not exactly sleeping together, but as good as.'

'It doesn't bother me,' she said stiffly, feeling colour creeping into her cheeks. 'I don't suppose I would have been hired if there were any anticipated problems.'

'Don't you believe it! Doctors are not exactly volunteering in droves to go up North. Maybe for a month or two in high summer. . .that's trendy. But not for six months. They want to get out before the really cold weather sets in come September. Even so, the NMDC don't usually put a man and a woman together unless they're married. That's asking for trouble.'

Although he kept his voice even, his words managed to sound insulting to her. Was this what she was to be up against, as well as the exigencies of the North? And she hadn't even landed in Yellowknife yet! Tim's forceful words echoed once more in her mind — 'merciless. . .arrogant. . .'

'If those remarks are intended as a put-down, Dr Bentall,' Alanna said firmly, with more cool than she felt, 'let me tell you now that I'm not easily put down. I don't see any problem with having to share living accommodation with a man — it's something I did at university from age eighteen, as well as on and off ever since. It's possible to be on a casual, friendly basis with someone of the opposite sex.' The unaccustomed primness of her tone did not sit well with her, yet her wide hazel eyes met his appraising grey ones unflinchingly.

'Sure,' he agreed, eyebrows raised slightly in amusement. 'It's a little different up North when you're thrown together with only a few other people you can talk to, who have anything in common with you. . .you can get very lonely. Especially when you're English, so far from home.'

'Yes, I understand that. I assume that we'll be working most of the time. . .exhausted when we're not.'

'Everyone needs some recreation, otherwise they burn out fast. Some women would take it as a compliment that I can anticipate problems.'

Alanna looked at him in surprise, finding herself wanting to laugh suddenly. 'I do believe you're an old-fashioned man, worried about quaint ideas of honour, and all that.' She smiled, unable to help herself. 'Don't worry, Dr Bentall, I'm quite capable of taking care of myself, of dealing with any man I don't find attractive or desirable. . .or of dealing with a man I do find attractive. So perhaps you are the one who should watch out. . .while I'm making up my mind.'

Her smile broadened. Gratified, she saw that he was evidently taken aback. 'I'm a modern woman, Dr Bentall, capable of taking the initiative if necessary. . . not just a passive object to be manipulated. If we start off on a professional basis, I'm sure we can take it from there. . .see which way the wind blows.'

She wasn't sure what had got into her; she just knew that she couldn't stop. A spark of anger, a disbelief, had given way to a wicked desire to call his bluff, to deflate his obvious ego and ready-made assumptions. She was no longer afraid. While he appeared temporarily speechless, their lunch arrived on little plastic trays covered with foil.

'May I call you Owen?' she added sweetly. 'And do

call me Alanna. . .please.' Her English accent sounded
clipped and precise compared with his flattened vowels
and rolled Rs. She hoped that she intimidated him. For
now, anyway. Not much hope of it lasting, though, she
knew instinctively. Any time soon he would no doubt
get a second wind.

They ate in silence. Alanna smiled to herself, while
he attacked his steak vigorously with an inadequate
plastic knife and fork. When they were at the coffee
stage he finally spoke again.

'So you're quite happy with the arrangement as it
stands?'

'Yes. . .quite.'

'It might be possible for some other arrangement to
be made once we get to Yellowknife. The NMDC has
an office there, as you will undoubtedly know. They
could maybe arrange some sort of switch. . .for some
other guy to go to Chalmers and you to stay in
Yellowknife, at the hospital there.'

'Why should I do that? I've come all the way from
England to go to Chalmers Bay. . .and that's where I'm
going. You could ask the people in Yellowknife,' she
added as an afterthought, 'to replace you. . .if you
would prefer not to be with me. I find it absolutely
incredible that you think it matters. Or is it pure
prejudice. . .?' Her voice trailed off. This was really a
strange conversation to be having with someone she
had only just met. Of all the contingencies she had
thought of, she had not considered prejudice.

'OK, OK,' he said, shrugging, smiling, spreading out
his hands in mock-surrender in the American manner,
'just trying to give you an "out", that's all. It's not
prejudice, I can assure you.'

'No? Well, then, Dr Bentall, you are just as free to
take the "out" as I am, especially as you were only hired

two days ago, while I applied for this job months ago. Because I was waiting for this, I didn't apply for any other post. So, frankly, I need the money. . .it's very well-paid, compared with England. It's not just the money, of course. . .it's a wonderful challenge. . .from a medical point of view and a personal one. . .to see the North.'

In the pause that followed, he looked at her, allowing his expression of cynicism to have its full effect on her. 'Don't forget,' he said succinctly, 'that I'm an old hand, while you have to learn the ropes. That will take time.'

'It's becoming rapidly apparent that you won't let me forget it. I'm a good doctor,' she said emphatically. 'North, south, east, or west. I've just spent a lot of time in a very busy trauma unit in a big hospital. I doubt that there's any type of injury that I haven't had to deal with, doing both surgery and anaesthesia. I understand that there's a lot of new oil exploration going on near Chalmers Bay, which is partly why two doctors have been hired. . .part of a new experimental scheme to deal with the inevitable trauma. . . I think I'm very well-qualified to deal with that, otherwise I would not have been hired.'

Before he could dispute her qualifications, she hurried on, wanting to make it quite clear from the outset that she was no dilettante, perhaps running away from so-called civilisation to escape personal problems. 'I've had obstetrics training, which will help in dealing with the local people. . .that was mandatory, as you know. I don't think there will be much "up North" that I can't cope with. Granted, you will have the edge over me in all that he-man stuff. . .but then the most experienced person will go out in the bush planes anyway for home visits, male or female. That's the standard procedure, I understand.'

'Point taken,' he said. 'However, we had another English doctor at Chalmers a year ago. . .he thought he could cope with anything and everything. . .then he found that he couldn't.'

That would be Tim, she thought bitterly. Dear, sweet Tim. . .

'He was a good guy, a good doctor,' Owen Bentall continued. 'He let himself down because he expected the equipment and the back-up services to be as good as they were in England. The trouble is, in the North there often is no back-up service whatsoever. . .the buck stops there. That's partly what the NMDC is all about, trying to improve the network of services to cover all the new industry up there, as well as the native people.'

Alanna had to bite her tongue in order not to interrupt, or to display any of the mounting anger that threatened her rather fragile poise. What he had said was not Tim's version of the story, and she had heard it first-hand from Tim many times.

'Were you working up there, then?' she asked, knowing the answer, wanting to hear what he would say.

'No. . .the other guy on the scene was Clinton Debray. . . I went up later when there were a few problems.' A thoughtful note in his voice suggested to Alanna, sensitive to any nuances, that he did not care very much for his erstwhile colleague Dr Debray.

At least he had something in common with Tim on that score. When Tim had come back to England after the inquiry, after the charge of professional negligence against him had been dropped, he had told her all about Clinton Debray who had been his co-partner at Chalmers Bay. An incompetent who drank too much. That had been his assessment. Unfortunately, Tim had been classed as the junior, being an outsider, and had been subjected to the other overriding his decisions. Tim had told her about Owen Bentall, too, how he had been sent up there to sort out the situation. . .

Now was the perfect moment to tell Owen Bentall that the English ˮdoctor he referred to was her half-brother, Tim Cooke, who was the reason in part why she herself was going to work at Chalmers Bay, with the same organisation that had employed Tim. Instinct urged her to remain silent. If she were to institute any behind-the-scenes enquiries of her own, to get more clearly at the truth of what had happened there, she was more likely to have success if her relationship to Tim remained unknown. There was nothing known by the organisation to connect the two of them.

'And you think I might fall into the same trap?' she asked coolly.

'It's a thought. Things can be primitive and tough up there.'

'So I've been told, *ad nauseam*. Battling with nature will be a refreshing change from battling with complex urban issues. Now, Dr Bentall,' she added sweetly, 'I suggest that we try to associate well together, to be co-operative, polite. . .all the things that the NMDC recommends in its guidelines for doctors.'

Abruptly she got up to go to the cloakroom, aware that her face was flushed. Behind the locked door of the tiny cloakroom she splashed cold water on her face. Her eyes, frustrated and angry, stared back at her from the mirror. With her sensitive colouring, her coppery red hair and pale skin that tended to freckle in the Celtic manner, any emotion generally brought a reveal-ing flush to her cheeks. Let him think she was a city girl who would fall flat on her face 'up North'. Life for her had been tough. It was obvious that Owen Bentall came from a wealthy background; perhaps he took it for

granted that she did too. Well. . .perhaps she was in a
better position to show him a thing or two. They would
have to start again from the beginning, she decided, if
they were to work together in any amicable way.

As she sank back into her seat, Owen Bentall held
out a hand to her, giving her a lazy, admiring smile,
letting his gaze go over her from her feet to her head,
lingering on her shining hair. His teeth were perfect and
very white. . .naturally, she noted with a renewed
cynicism, at the same time as she felt herself succumb-
ing swiftly to his attraction.

'Let's start again, shall we?' he said. 'From the
beginning?' His eyes met hers and held her gaze. 'What
do you say to that?'

Alanna took the hand, nonplussed. He seemed to
have pre-empted her. 'Yes. . .yes, of course.'

The hand that lay warmly in his tingled with the
shock of contact. Slowly she withdrew it, settling herself
comfortably in her reclining seat, closing her eyes. They
had done enough talking for now. Quite suddenly she
was intensely sensitised to his close proximity in a new
way. A niggling thought entered her mind reluctantly.
Perhaps there was something relevant, after all, about
his reservations. . .

Turning her head away from him, she willed herself
to relax, to doze. Eventually the aircraft began its
barely perceptible descent.

'Attention please, ladies and gentlemen,' the voice of
a flight attendant, chirpy with a professional friendli-
ness, came again over the intercom. 'We shall very
shortly be landing at Yellowknife Airport. Please
ensure that your hand baggage is securely stowed under
the seat in front of you and fasten seatbelts. We thank
you for flying First Nation Air and welcome you to the
Land of the Midnight Sun.'

behind her. Although she did not look up she knew it was him, knew his was the warm hand that rested briefly on her upper arm when she took an unconscionably long time to count the heart-rate.

'Having trouble locating the foetal heart, Dr Hargrove?' There was amusement in his laconic drawl and, it seemed to her sensitised ears, another insinuation.

'No. . .no. Just taking my time, that's all, as Lynne's my last patient.' She wished he would not touch her. Slowly she straightened up, removing the stethoscope. The cubicle was too small for the three of them; he was big as well as tall. Even when Alanna pressed herself back against the wall so that he could see their patient his shoulder brushed hers.

'Hi, Lynne!' he said. 'I heard you say my name, Alanna. Everything OK? Blood-pressure?'

'Yes, it's normal. She was wondering whether she really has to go down to the city later on when the baby's due, or whether she could have the Caesarian section here, if it's necessary.'

His hand brushed hers as he took the chart from her. 'And what did you tell her?' he asked smoothly, flipping through the pages.

'You have already suggested that she should go. . . you saw her last; I'm referring her to you.'

'Mm. . .ah, yes. . . I remember. You had an obstructed labour last time, Lynne.' He looked at Alanna. 'There's about a ninety-five per cent chance that it would happen again, I should think. There was disproportion. . .a transverse lie.' He turned his attention again to the young woman on the couch. 'We could certainly do the operation here, but if anything special is needed for the baby, or if it's premature, we wouldn't do so well up here with equipment and staff. Everything would be fine, of course, but the baby might be somewhat better off in a neonatal unit, with a paediatrician.'

'Oh.' The young woman was clearly not happy.

'We'll see.' Owen smiled at Lynne. 'Not to worry about it now. You get dressed. Come back to the clinic in two weeks' time; we'll talk about it some more then. The baby isn't big enough yet for us to tell much about its final size, or its future position in the uterus. OK?'

'Yes. Thank you, doctor.'

Alanna helped her patient off the couch, then was alone with her colleague when Lynne returned to the dressing cubicle where she had left her outdoor clothing.

'I don't bite, Alanna. You don't have to cower against the wall like that.' He grinned now, showing again those perfect teeth, as though to demonstrate that he was not capable of biting her with them.

'I'm not so sure,' she countered. 'And I don't cower.'

'Here.' He gave her back the chart. 'Write up your notes. Don't forget to sign them, and every entry you make. . .we need that for any—er—legal matters that could possibly arise from our work here. Keep that in mind whenever you write anything; it helps to protect us too, as well as the patients. Always make thorough notes. Then I'll meet you over in our sitting-room for tea. You can go over the day's cases with me there.'

To her consternation, he stood next to her and watched while she charted Lynne Nanchook's blood-pressure, her weight, the results of her haemoglobin and urine tests, the size of her uterus, the foetal heart-rate.

'Would you say that her due date of delivery is correct according to uterus size?' he queried her abruptly. 'And what is your opinion about sending her to the city?'

Without definite reason she felt herself becoming flustered under his intense scrutiny that seemed to burn right through her, aware that her hand had not been steady as he had watched her write. Damn him!

'I. . . I. . .' she began to stammer, then corrected herself. 'The uterus is the right size for the dates she has given for her last menstrual period. As for whether she should stay here. . .it will be summer. . .but I would rather defer to your judgement until I know this place better.'

'What if you didn't have me to defer to?' he said harshly.

'Then I would send her. . .of course,' she admitted, feeing that he had somehow trapped her.

'Go off duty now,' he said, in a brisk, dismissive tone that brooked no contradiction as he plucked the chart from her fingers and swung on his heel away from her out of the cubicle. 'I'll see you over there for tea.'

Not wanting the clinic nurse to see her flushed face, she walked quickly to the door to the covered walkway that linked the clinic to the medical staff living quarters, collecting her coat from a hook beside the door as she passed. She was still counting the time in hours that she had been at the clinic, yet by all that she had absorbed so far it seemed like weeks. She pondered over this as she entered the chill of the passage.

The sitting-room was quiet. Someone had placed sandwiches on a table, and there was a vacuum jug of tea. Alanna sat down and closed her eyes, resting her head back against the chair, desperately tired. The confusion that she had felt on the journey northwards about what Owen Bentall really thought of her was back in full force. . .and what she thought of him. None the less, it had been a good day, with the antenatal clinic in the afternoon, a paediatric clinic in the morning.

Although the last lap of the journey up there was only yesterday, already it was taking on the semblance of a dream. She let her thoughts wander back over what had taken place. . . When they had landed at Yellowknife the air had been crisp, dry and quite cold, even though the sun had been bright. Yet it was nowhere near as cold as up here, where the wind moaned around the buildings, lifting the dry surface snow in swirling eddies.

Just before landing at Yellowknife they had flown over the enormous expanse of Great Slave Lake, much of which was still frozen over, and Owen Bentall had pointed it out to her, together with a few other landmarks in the vast territory that was largely uninhabited, much of it still under snow. The city, on the northern edge of the lake, still shivered in the transitional stage from winter to summer. Huge mounds of dirty snow had lined the edges of the runway. They were to stay in Yellowknife for the rest of the day to pick up a few supplies and some necessary Arctic clothing for her, spend the night there, then head out the next day for Chalmers Bay on a chartered plane. Everything had been arranged for them ahead of time by the NMDC.

Alanna had looked around her with interest. Things were so different from anything she had seen before. Everything manmade had a functional, utilitarian look about it, set down rather incongruously in the wilderness. The land around them was mainly flat, with few trees. She had begun then to get a feeling of the vastness of the land and the distance that they had yet to travel. The town had a frontier atmosphere, a sense of urgency and energy.

'The Medical Corps is very efficient, isn't it?' she had said brightly.

'Yeah, it is. . .usually,' he had replied.

The sound of a slamming door brought her mentally back to the present and to the physical reality of the medical station.

'Hi! Sorry to be so long.' The object of her thoughts stood before her in the flesh, enveloped in an enormous parka of the type that she had been supplied with in Yellowknife. 'I decided to go out for a quick walk, once around the block, for some fresh air.' He shrugged off the massive padded coat. 'You haven't had anything to eat yet! Are you OK, Alanna? Not suffering from too much jet-lag, I hope? Hmm?' As he sat opposite her to pull off the heavy boots that he wore he fixed her with the intent gaze that was beginning to affect her in an as yet undefinable way, his concern obviously genuine.

'Just very tired. . .otherwise all right.' Her attempt at lightness did not quite come off, when he so dominated the room.

'Stay sitting; I'll get you some tea. Then I suggest an early night. You'll have to remind me that I'm being an insensitive clod if I seem to push you too hard.' He handed her a steaming mug of tea. 'Sugar?'

'Please.' If he was as aware as she was of the intense undercurrents between them he was managing to hide it very well. It was her first instinct to ask him outright whether he had revised his opinion about living with a woman in the short time that they had been there, but could not find suitable words for an opening sentence.

'I tend to push myself, because there's so much to accomplish up here, and I tend to do the same to others,' he said. 'Tell me what you thought of today. Sandwich?'

'Thanks. Well. . . I enjoyed the day. As I expected, there were a lot of respiratory infections in the children. I was wondering whether tuberculosis is a problem.'

'Yes. . .unfortunately there seems to be a new upsurge. . .a type resistant to the usual drugs. So we have to try to spot it early, with routine chest X-rays, and so on.'

'I see. . .'

For a long time they talked, all through tea, then through supper later, managing to keep the topic strictly business.

In bed later that night, cosy and warm, feeling the wind buffeting the building in which she lay, she found herself once again going over all that had happened, sorting and sifting.

It had been a Twin Otter, painted bright red and white, that was waiting to fly them to Chalmers Bay the next morning when they had woken in Yellowknife. There were smaller planes equipped with skis instead of wheels that stood beside it, reminding them that they were flying to an area where winter still reigned, where the temperature would be about minus five degress Celsius and where it would reach only a maximum of about nine degrees in the middle of summer. The pilot of the charter company, wearing a blue flight suit, had met them by the plane. 'Hi,' he greeted them. 'You the guys going to Chalmers?'

'Hi,' Owen Bentall returned the greeting. 'Yes, that's us.'

'OK, just leave your gear there. I'll be back in a tick to stow it,' came the laconic reply, at odds with the excitement that once again gripped Alanna in the pit of the stomach.

Alanna was wearing a warm jacket and trousers, and carrying the heavy parka, its hood trimmed with wolf fur, that she had picked up from the outfitters the day before. 'I've never been on a plane this small.' She smiled up at Owen Bentall, determined to be friendly. He looked very tall and big in the heavy clothing that he wore, masculine and attractive. I bet he knows it too, she found herself thinking.

'It's noisy. . .pretty bumpy at times while you're in the air; the landings can be rough, particularly if we have to put down in an emergency in a place where there's no landing strip.' He turned astute grey eyes on her, unsmiling, as though he was assessing whether she was likely to survive the flight. 'It's quite safe. . .so not to worry.' His drawling voice held a hint of mockery. Although he gave her a ghost of a smile then, she had the distinct feeling that he intended to hold her at arm's length, so to speak. Well, that was all right with her. . .

'I see,' she said, determined not to let him see how nervous she really was.

'This will be a good trial for you,' he went on. 'When we have to go out on bush flights, or a medivac — that's the transfer of a patient by air back here to Yellowknife — we often have to go on either a Twin Otter or a Cessna. . .that's a single-engine light plane.'

'Yes. . . I see,' she said again, not caring to inform him at this stage that she already knew all that, had read all the very thorough information that had been sent to her in England before she had even accepted the job. She knew what she was getting into all right. . .at least, in theory.

The plane was even noisier than she had expected. Conversation was impossible because of it, plus the fact that they sat in single file, with a few other passengers, down one side of the plane, with their baggage, a large oil drum and other odd assorted items strapped down at the rear and the other side of the cabin. Owen sat in front of her, his large presence offering her a certain reassurance.

She had a wonderful view from her window. The barrens stretched out below them like a giant jigsaw puzzle, with lakes of all imaginable shapes and sizes, their ice floes gleaming in the sunlight. There were clusters of spruce trees, partially frozen rivers, patches of brown vegetation emerging from the melting snow. Very soon all human habitation was lost to view. Between here and Chalmers Bay there were no roads, no railways, no people apart from the few who manned the weather stations along the route, to monitor climatic conditions and maintain radio contact with air traffic. After what seemed like an interminable journey, the plane suddenly dropped down to land at the first weather station, situated beside a lake.

Stiff with inaction and cold, they all clumsily negotiated the rickety metal steps to get out. Two of the men were to stay here and, with the pilot's help, begin to unload their gear.

'We'll be staying here for about half an hour, folks,' the pilot called to them, 'so stretch your legs, use the washrooms, get a snack from the kitchen in there — they'll have something ready for us.' The drop in temperature, after Yellowknife, was immediately apparent.

'I feel like a zombie in this parka. . .these heavy boots.' Alanna laughed, clumping over to stand beside Owen. There was no way that she would admit to him that she also felt a little out of place, being the only woman here in this remote spot that was very obviously a strongly male preserve.

Her observation was confirmed when the man who

was putting out the food grinned at her almost shyly. 'Don't get too many women here,' he said, 'except once in a while when Bonnie Mae's passing through this way.'

Alanna smiled back, accepting a mug of hot chocolate that Owen passed to her. 'Help yourself to sandwiches,' he said. His manner seemed to alternate between being protective or aloof where she was concerned.

'Thank you. Just what I need. Who's Bonnie Mae?'

'She's the nurse where we're going. . .a great girl. She's been up at Chalmers, on and off, for about three years. . .seems to have taken to the place like a natural. But then she would, I guess, seeing that she was born in Edmonton. They have pretty awful winters there too . . .lots of snow.' From the way his face lit up, the warmth in his voice, he obviously thought a lot of Bonnie Mae. Alanna had a mental vision of the nurse, a voluptuous, curvy blonde with baby-blue eyes, full, pouting lips, very much in love with the attractive Dr Bentall. . .

'The place at Chalmers used to be just a nursing station,' he interrupted her reverie, 'before all the oil exploration got going in the Beaufort Sea and elsewhere in the area. Bonnie Mae coped with the place single-handed. . .coped with absolutely everything that came in, made all the decisions. A terrific girl and a really good nurse.'

The vision renewed itself in Alanna's mind as she took a hearty mouthful of a sandwich. Not only was Bonnie Mae good to look at, she had a sexy walk, flawless complexion, long eyelashes that fluttered agitatedly when she looked at Dr Bentall. Perhaps that was why he was not too keen on having another woman up there; it might interfere with his ongoing amour. . .

'Another sandwich, Alanna?' He was looking at her quizzically. 'Is something amusing you?'

'Oh. . .yes. . .thank you.' She took a sandwich. 'I mean. . .no——' She broke off confusedly, a flush spreading over her cheeks. 'It's getting awfully hot in this parka.' She drew down the heavy zip. To her annoyance, he still watched her.

'You look very cute when you blush,' he said, surprisingly. 'I wonder what you were thinking about?'

'Nothing much. . .' The noise of conversation in the room seemed suddenly stilled as her mind blotted it out, as her eyes met his and held. He looked at her intently, she felt, as though really seeing her for the first time.

'Hey, Owen. . .' Mercifully, one of the other men, who obviously knew him, came up to them to engage her colleague in conversation.

Moving away from them, she looked out of the window at their plane on the makeshift landing strip, aware that her heart was beating unnaturally fast and that, without really knowing why, her relationship with Owen Bentall had undergone a subtle change. A change that engendered feelings of both anticipation and an unfamiliar apprehension.

The pilot came into the room, zipping up his flight suit. 'All ready to go, folks!' he bawled. 'Let's move it!'

The ongoing passengers trooped out once again to the aircraft. The next stop would be above latitude sixty, above the Arctic Circle.

Very much later Alanna was aware of someone shaking her shoulder. Her head had fallen sideways to rest against the wall of the cabin.

'Wake up!' Owen Bentall was sitting on the side of his seat looking at her. 'Had a good sleep?'

'Yes. Oh. . . I'm so stiff.' She stretched out as much as she could in the cramped space. 'Where are we?'

'Almost at Chalmers,' he said. 'We'll be coming in to land very soon.'

'It's still so bright!' she exclaimed enthusiastically, looking out of the window at the snow-covered tundra beneath them, a vast whiteness as far as the eye could see, with the sky looking like a huge blue dome above them. They had to shout to make themselves heard.

'Yes, they have practically eighteen hours of daylight here now. . .after twenty-four-hour darkness for much of the winter.'

'It's amazing!' Down below them the buildings of Chalmers Bay came into view, tiny dots in the sea of white, single-storey buildings connected to each other by wires on utility poles. Alanna could see a small wooden church, with a cross atop a tiny spire. She wondered which building was the medical station. So this place, this wilderness, was to be her home for the next six months. There was a certain comfort in the knowledge that Tim had been here before her.

The pilot turned to look at them over his shoulder through the open door of the cockpit. 'We're going down, folks,' he bawled. 'Strap yourselves in and secure all bags.' They heard him make contact with the control tower at the airstrip, then the plane began to dip down, circling in a wide arc over the village.

Alanna knew, from having studied maps of the area in great detail, that Chalmers Bay, designated as a village, was situated on the edge of Coronation Gulf, a channel that went west into the Beaufort Sea and the Arctic Ocean, then the Pacific Ocean. Then to the east and north it continued round many frozen, inhospitable islands to come out eventually in the Atlantic Ocean. From the Twin Otter she could see the frozen water of the bay. A large ship that looked like an ice-breaker lay at anchor in part of a strip of water in which floated chunks of ice.

Quite quickly they were down. The pilot made an expert landing beside the tiny airport building and control tower. Alanna felt a surge of admiration for the laconic pilot, whom she only knew as Rick, who must have to cope with emergencies of various types almost every day of his life.

The luggage was unloaded directly on to the frozen snow. Two men came towards them on skidoos, motorised sledges on skis, each one pulling a cart on which to load the luggage to transport it inside. The air was clear, dry, and very cold.

'Come inside. We'll pick up our bags there. Someone will be there to meet us with some sort of vehicle.' Owen spoke easily, obviously very relaxed and familiar with the routine, as he casually zipped up his parka. The snow squeaked under foot as they walked the short distance to the building. The sunlight was almost blinding as it was reflected off the snow. Alanna fumbled in her handbag for the dark glasses that she had been advised to bring to guard against the snow blindness that could come from over-exposure to the brilliant light. There were few people around. Three children stood near the building, obviously having come to watch the arrival of the plane. They were Eskimo, or Inuit as the native people preferred to be called. They looked adorable in their hooded anoraks.

'Hello, Dr Bentall. It's good to see you again. You weren't expecting to be up here again so soon, eh?' The speaker was a young native man who had come up to them as soon as they were inside, smiling shyly.

'Hello, Skip. It's good to see you too, although I do admit that I'd much rather be in Barbados right now.

Nothing personal.' Owen Bentall laughed ruefully as he shook hands with the young man. 'Skip, this is Dr Alanna Hargrove. . . Alanna, this is Skip, alias Skipper, alias something else unpronounceable. . . which is why he's called Skip.'

'Hello. . .pleased to meet you.' She smiled, taking his hand.

'Skip works at the medical station,' Owen explained. 'He's a scrub technician in the operating-room, does a bit of radiography and dozens of other extremely useful jobs.'

Skip smiled quietly at this description. 'I've got the pick-up truck outside, Dr Bentall.' The three of them carried the bags and other equipment, including boxes of fresh fruit and vegetables that they had bought in Yellowknife, out to the pick-up truck, which proved to be a battered vehicle with enormous snow tyres. It was evident, from a cursory inspection of the village, that apart from the ubiquitous skidoos there were very few other types of vehicles. They would have been useless, since there were no roads out of the community.

The medical station was at the other end of the village, next to open tundra. There were no trees. Alanna had read that here they were just beyond the treeline, an area beyond which no trees would grow because of the intense cold for much of the year. Instead, there was some scrub, mosses, lichens and some Arctic flowers which bloomed and reproduced furiously in the short summer before cold and darkness descended again.

The medical station was made up of several metal-clad portables, rather like large holiday caravans put together, and like many other buildings in the village. They were connected by enclosed walkways which, Alanna supposed, were to enable them to move easily from one to another during bad weather without having to put on heavy clothing to go outside.

'I'll take the luggage in, Dr Bentall,' Skip offered, when they had come to a halt outside a large portable, 'if you want to go into the clinic to say hello to Bonnie Mae. She's just dying to meet Dr Hargrove. It's going to be a great treat for her to have a woman doctor here for a change. Then we've got dinner for you. We'll serve it in your place as soon as you're ready.'

'Thanks, Skip.' A warm smile lit up Owen Bentall's handsome face, momentarily easing the tiredness there. 'And I can't wait to get my arms around Bonnie Mae!'

Alanna felt a stab of irritation mingling with the fatigue that now threatened to overwhelm her. It was not at all clear why her colleague had been so averse to having a female partner when there was a female nurse here anyway, one whom he obviously liked very much. Perhaps that, in itself, was the reason. . .

They proceeded up a wooden ramp to enter one of the other buildings that was marked 'clinic'. Inside, everything appeared neat, compact, well-organised, and smelled of antiseptic. There was a small waiting-room to one side of the door, while several small rooms opposite were clearly treatment- and storage-rooms. Owen led the way quietly along the short corridor.

'Owen Bentall!' The sound came from behind them, what could only be described as a screech. 'You old son-of-a-gun!' Owen spun round. Alanna turned more slowly.

Bonnie Mae was enormously fat. She stood before them like an advertisement for sumptuous good living. The vision that Alanna had manufactured of blonde, blue-eyed beauty disintegrated and disappeared for-ever. The nurse wore a pale pink uniform trouser suit of gigantic proportions, the trousers straining tightly over heavy thighs, rolls of fat scarcely disguised beneath the shirt-like top. She was pretty, her plump, child-like face wreathed by a halo of light brown hair, her eyes a darker brown; her cheeks dimpled when she smiled. Around her neck, with a stethoscope, she wore a gold chain on which hung a large diamond solitaire ring.

'Let me give you a hug, you old devil!' With that, she flung her ample arms around Owen Bentall, squeezing him tightly. To Alanna's amazement, he didn't seem to mind but simply hugged her in return.

'A little less of the "old", Bonnie Mae.' He was laughing.

'And you are Dr Hargrove.' Bonnie Mae turned her attention to Alanna, who was barely controlling a hysterical desire to laugh. The contrast between the Owen Bentall she was seeing now and the studiously polite man who had had supper with her the previous evening in Yellowknife was almost too great to comprehend. 'It's so great to meet you! You've no idea how I've looked forward to this. . .to actually have a woman here. I've been outnumbered for so long.'

'Hello. I'm pleased to meet you, and I'll do my very best to live up to your expectations.'

'Your accent! I just love that accent! Just like that cute Dr Cooke; unfortunately I only got to work with him for a short while. . . I was away on vacation. Now, we're going to get along just fine, Dr Hargrove. May I call you Alanna?' They shook hands.

'Yes. . .please do.'

'Great! Dr Bentall here I just refer to as "Doc". . . with a capital D, of course. You're even more beautiful than I had pictured. . .red hair! And lovely hazel eyes. You had better watch out, Doc.' She turned to Owen Bentall with a wink. 'Over there in that little annexe with this lovely girl, you might be tempted.' While

Bonnie Mae laughed at her own wit, Alanna cast a somewhat alarmed glance at the man who was the object of her innuendo. Surely now the nurse had gone too far. She felt herself beginning to blush.

'I might, at that, Bonnie,' he said, still grinning. 'You've made Alanna blush.'

'Oh, don't mind me! It helps to be a bit crazy up here . . .it keeps you sane, if you know what I mean. And I'm the craziest of the lot. Now, you folks must be really tired and hungry. We'll leave the guided tour for tomorrow. Everything's ready for you over in the annexe. The cook will bring over your dinner any time now. He got the steaks out of the ice-box as soon as he heard the plane come in. Now, Alanna, you take care and I'll see you tomorrow; have a good meal and sleep tight. It's better to rest up before you do any sightseeing. And don't let that guy bully you. . .he does sometimes, you know.'

'So I've found out,' Alanna ventured, not looking at her colleague.

'Right on! I see you've got his number! Actually, he's a great guy most of the time.' She looked at her watch. 'I'm expecting two patients any time now, so I'll say bye; see you later.'

They walked to their quarters through the covered walkway, which had a door and a window set into it, then double doors leading into their annexe, obviously to help keep out the cold. 'That's Bonnie Mae,' Owen said, with a lop-sided smile, looking at her closely for her reaction.

'Does she always talk in superlatives?'

'A good deal of the time. She's a great nurse, very calm and efficient. That's the main thing. . .plus the fact that her sense of humour keeps us all going.'

The living quarters were not quite what Alanna had

expected from Owen Bentall's description. Granted, the place was cramped, but it was all very well-organised for the best use of space, very functional, yet with a number of homely touches that had obviously been left behind by previous occupants. Alanna stood in the small living-cum-dining-room looking at the colourful pictures and prints that had been put up on the walls, and postcards that were pinned to a cork noticeboard, wondering whether any of them had been Tim's.

Next to the living-room was a tiny galley-type kitchen, equipped with all sorts of gadgets, including a microwave oven. Through a doorway she saw her luggage in a neat pile. That was her bedroom. To her surprise, and relief, she had her own tiny bathroom off her bedroom. There was even a small laundry, with automatic washer and drier. They might be hundreds of miles away from so-called civilisation, but North Americans had to have their gadgets if they could possibly manage it.

She wandered out again to the living-room, quite satisfied with everything, even with the lock on her door. There was a radio telephone in the living area and an intercom telephone in the bedroom.

'See what I mean?' Owen came in to join her. 'Scarcely room to swing a cat.'

'I don't intend to swing any cats. To me this is almost palatial. I don't come from a wealthy background.' It was time to disabuse him. 'I've lived in some really crummy flats in my time. I'm used to hardship.'

'Good. Your experience will no doubt be put to good use here. Excuse me while I have a shower,' he said crisply, his previous good humour giving way to something more formal. 'Our dinner should be delivered in about ten minutes. There's a cook here, part-time. We can either order food in advance from the kitchen, or cook for ourselves here.' He was gone quickly, shutting the door of his room behind him with a sharp, dismissive click.

She went thoughtfully to her room, feeling immense relief at having actually arrived. Everything, she felt, was going to be all right after all. Both Bonnie Mae and Skip, from first impressions, seemed as though they would be good to work with. No doubt a routine would be sorted out between all of them for maximum efficiency.

It seemed like a luxury to take off the heavy clothing, to have a hot, relaxing shower. While she was dressing again she heard the cook come in with their dinner and engage in conversation with Owen. This is what it must have been like for Tim, a year ago. How difficult things must have gradually become for him with a partner like Dr Clinton Debray, who, it appeared, was something of a misfit wherever he went. Even with the underlying hostility that emanated from Owen Bentall, she knew that she was luckier in her colleague than her brother had been in his. Also, she had had the benefit of a warning. Forewarned was forearmed.

Dressed in casual leggings in a bright yellow colour, with a matching heavy sweatshirt, she went out to the living area to find her partner putting cutlery and plates out on a small table for them.

'What can I do?' she offered brightly.

'You could bring out the food from the oven. . .it's a traditional Canadian meal, you might say: grilled steak, baked potatoes and sweet corn, even though the sweet corn was frozen.' As he spoke, his eyes went over her quickly, appraisingly, from head to foot and back again. He looked more relaxed too, in an open-neck checked shirt and jeans.

Alanna carried the food out to the table. 'This smells wonderful. . .makes me realise how ravenous I am. One probably gets hungrier up here in the cold.'

'Yes, one does. Hence the size of Bonnie Mae. It's partly boredom too, of course, up here in the winter, with not much to do in your off time except eat and watch television. Thank God for the satellite.' There was a certain insinuation in his voice as he gave her a long, considering look. She knew what he was thinking . . .that a man and a woman thrown together in such close proximity would soon find things to do for recreation, other than eating, in the long, dark days of winter. She felt herself tense with a sharp awareness of him.

'Would you like red wine with the meal?' he asked, still looking at her. 'I brought a few bottles with me.'

'Yes, that would be lovely. Perhaps you could fill me in on a few details of the job while we eat, so that I won't have too many surprises. If you don't mind talking shop, that is.'

'Sure,' he said, opening the wine bottle expertly. 'Sit down, help yourself. Leave some room for the hot apple pie and whipped cream.'

The steak was excellent. As Alanna ate, she looked around the room, noting the video machine under the television, with a pile of video tapes next to it. There were books, mostly paperbacks, filling a bookcase, a compact-disc player and a radio. The small room was basic but comfortable.

'We're pretty well-supplied here,' Owen commented, following her observations. 'All the guys who come up here bring something, then leave it for the next lot.'

'That's a good way of doing things —— ' She broke off as her gaze travelled over the window. 'Oh. . .it's snowing!' Through the small triple-glazed window they could see flakes of snow swirling against the building.

'It won't last long. From now on things will be getting steadily warmer. The weather can change, though, very quickly, at any time of the year. That's why you always have to be prepared; never go away from shelter without proper clothing. Or without a rifle.'

'A rifle?'

'Polar bears come into the community, trying to get at the garbage dumps. They're a nuisance. . .dangerous. We carry rifles to scare them off, we rarely have to shoot one. There are rangers up here who deal with them.' Then he was grinning at her. 'Your eyes have grown as big as saucers. Not to worry too much. We keep two rifles right here. I'll show you them tomorrow, perhaps give you a few shooting lessons. Or perhaps you already know how to shoot?' By the way he said it he evidently did not expect her to answer in the affirmative.

'As a matter of fact, I do,' she said, looking him full in the face challengingly, warmed by the wine. 'I have a cousin who's an expert shot. He taught me.'

'No kidding! Then perhaps you can help me to improve my aim. I wonder what other things you can teach me, Dr Hargrove?' The slow smile he gave her would have melted the heart of the most ardent man-hater, and she certainly was not that.

'Quite a lot, I should imagine. Now, how about some apple pie?' She gathered up their empty plates. 'Then perhaps we can talk shop.'

'Sure,' he replied lazily, lounging back in his chair while she brought in their next course, 'then I'll make the coffee. Let me see. . .where shall I start? Well, first thing in the morning I'll show you around more. There's the main reception area that you saw just now, with the waiting-room and treatment-rooms for outpatients, then through one of the other walkways there's an operating-room. . .basic but quite adequate. With the two of us here now we can deal with emergencies that have to be operated on, like acute appendicitis, et cetera, that would have had to be flown out before.'

'That must have been risky in some cases,' she ventured.

'Yes, it was. However, it wasn't cost-effective, before all the mining up here, to do otherwise.'

'What about major trauma?' she asked. 'And blood for transfusions?'

'We deal with trauma in the first instance, then we ship them out. There's no blood bank here as such, of course. We have blood for emergencies, and some frozen plasma. . .it's all shipped up from Yellowknife. Do you know how to type and cross-match blood?'

'Yes.'

'Good,' he said briskly. 'You're going to need that. Coffee?'

'Please.' While he had been talking she had gained some idea of what a task master and perfectionist he could be, not someone who would be tolerant of stupidity. In a way she was glad of that; there wouldn't be much room for error in a place like this. Tim had found that out. Unfortunately, remote places like this did not necessarily attract the best doctors. Owen Bentall, her intuition told her, would prove to be an exception.

They continued to talk for some time, until at last Owen stood up, stretching languidly. 'Since it's our first day tomorrow, we'll make a late start, about nine-thirty, to get over the effects of the journey. Don't bother to clear anything away; someone will come in tomorrow early to fix it.'

'Thank you for all the information. . .and for the wine; I enjoyed it. I hope you'll find me more of an asset than you originally thought.'

'You asked me on the plane if you could call me Owen. . .yes, you can. As for whether you will be an asset, it's up to you to prove yourself, isn't it?'

'I shall do my best. The other question is, will you be an asset to me? Goodnight. . . Owen.'

That had been yesterday. Now, snuggling down further into the warm bed, another evening over, Alanna knew the answer to that question after her first working day at Chalmers Bay. Owen Bentall was definitely going to be an asset to her as a medical colleague, once she had earned his trust. As for anything else, only time would tell.

CHAPTER THREE

'AND this is where we keep the non-current patient records, going back over the last five years.' Owen Bentall rested a hand for a moment on the door of a tall cupboard in the office of the clinic when they were doing a more comprehensive tour of the medical station on her second working day there.

So that was where any records would be, Alanna noted silently, pertaining to the case that had got her brother into trouble. . .unless they had been removed by the authorities. Tim had told her most of the details, but she wanted to read the chart anyway. Not wanting to display an undue interest, she moved on. The whole place was basic, yet adequate, as Owen had said, for anything they were likely to encounter. As Alanna looked around she was impressed by the understated efficiency of it all.

'We try to keep our use of disposable equipment to a minimum here. For one thing it's expensive to get it here, for another it presents problems of disposal.'

'I'm impressed,' she said.

'Good,' he said, looking at her sharply. 'A lot of people start bitching as soon as they get here about the lack of some very particular pieces of equipment that they have come to rely on and that are missing here. People who can't adapt or be innovative are pretty useless up here.' This morning he looked very much in character, in a green two-piece scrub suit under a white lab coat, a functional outfit that matched her own. The tan, she noticed, was already fading. He looked very masculine and powerful, even a little intimidating. 'Come on, I'll show you the defibrillator and the emergency drugs that we use for a cardiac arrest. Later on today you'll have time to go over all that stuff, to have a look at the anaesthetic machines, to find out exactly where everything's kept. Bonnie Mae will doubtless go over it all again.'

'Thank you.' At this stage she preferred to look and listen, only asking the most pertinent questions. It was not her style to come on too strong in the beginning, to try to assert herself before she had really got the basic hang of the place. Besides, he seemed to be making up for lost time.

Later, in the small ward area which contained beds, each one partitioned off at the sides, they found Skip admitting a patient, an elderly Inuit man whose weathered face was so criss-crossed with wrinkles that it looked like a dried apple, the like of which Alanna had only seen in photographs.

'Morning, Skip. This is the guy for the toe amputation, eh?'

'That's right, Dr Bentall. When do you think you'll be ready to do it?'

'Oh. . .any time you can have the operating-room ready, Skip. There's no rush, seeing as Bonnie Mae's out doing house calls. Dr Hargrove is going to do it. We'll just give him a bit of local anaesthetic, then he can go home later. OK, Alanna?' It was not really a question to which she had a choice. He deliberately kept his handsome face bland as he looked at her.

'Um. . .yes,' she said. That was the first she had heard of it. He was going to throw her in at the deep end, she could see that, to test her out early and quickly, then perhaps try to get rid of her if, in his estimation, she did not measure up. Well, a toe amputation was nothing. Life would be pretty boring very quickly if that was the average of what she would have to deal with. She smiled warmly at the three men, letting her attention come to rest on the patient. 'Good morning,' she added, for his benefit.

'He only speaks the local lingo, Inuktitut,' Owen informed her, 'of which there are several dialects.' Perhaps to impress her, he launched into a brief conversation with the old man.

'You're absolutely amazing, Dr Bentall!' she said in mock-awe.

'Before you think me too insufferable, I've only memorised a few pat words and phrases that one generally needs to know around here for purposes of taking a medical history. Skip can do all the interpreting we need. Most of the middle-aged and younger Inuit speak English, of course. Now, I think I've shown you just about everything for the time being. How about a cup of coffee? Then Skip can call us when the OR's ready. OK, Skip?'

'Sure, Dr Bentall.'

'Come on, we'll go back to the office to make coffee. Anything else you want to know?' He set a brisk pace, white coat flapping, as they returned to the clinic area where there was an automatic coffee-maker.

'Not for the moment. . . I think I've got enough buzzing around in my head to assimilate for now.'

He busied himself making coffee for them. 'This afternoon, when Bonnie Mae's back, I'll take you out on the clinic's skidoo to show you the community. Dress warmly, in a full snow suit and mukluks. Those things are hellishly cold.'

About half an hour later, after she had examined their patient, Mr Qitdlarssuaq, she went to the ante-room by the main operating-room to tie on a face mask, then wash her hands and arms at the sink. Owen strolled in casually to watch her, his dark hair covered with a green cotton operating cap. Nonchalantly he took a mask from the box and tied it over his nose and mouth. 'We elected to go on using washable masks here, instead of the disposables,' he said. He lounged against the sink. 'I won't scrub with you, I'll just hang around to help, since Bonnie isn't back yet.'

And to watch me like a hawk, she smiled to herself, glad that the expression on her face was at least partially hidden by the mask and her headgear. 'Does my scrub technique meet with your approval so far?' she asked, busily soaping her arms with the liquid Betadine solution.

'Mm-hmm,' he said. He continued to watch her, while she suppressed growing feelings of annoyance, trying to keep a calm exterior when she was becoming more and more sensitised to his presence. Above the sink was a clock. Every few seconds she glanced at it, wanting to be sure that she scrubbed for the required number of minutes, not wanting to give him the slightest opportunity to find fault with her, even in the most petty things. If he had chosen to put her on trial, unoffficially, she would do the same to him. Anything he did that she didn't approve of would be brought to his attention if he made life difficult for her.

Skip was waiting for her with a sterile towel and gown when she went, with hands and arms dripping, into the operating-room. He had already scrubbed well ahead of her to prepare his instruments and sterile drapes. When she had dried her skin he held the gown for her so that she had simply to push her arms into it.

'Let me tie you up,' Owen's drawling voice murmured behind her and she felt his fingers touch her back through the thin cotton of her scrub suit as he tied the back-ties on her gown. He seemed to be taking an unnecessarily long time about it. 'I'll bring in the patient now,' he added. 'I'll be the porter and the general go-fer. Anything you want, just say the word, Alanna.'

'I will, don't worry!' She forced a lightness into her voice. The operation did not concern her one bit; she knew she could do it with one hand tied behind her back. What did worry her was Owen Bentall. Skip held each sterile glove open for her to slip a hand into it. She squared her shoulders and put her head up. Now she was quite ready.

'Right,' she said to Skip.

'Would you take a look at the instruments, Dr Hargrove, to see that I've got everything you'll need? And what sutures do you like? We have a pretty good selection here.'

'Well. . .let me see.' As she looked, Owen wheeled in their patient, whom they referred to as 'Mr Q', and soon had him positioned on the operating table. Alanna felt herself warming more and more to Skip, with his pleasant manner and quiet, unassuming efficiency. Apparently he was not a fully registered nurse, but a registered nursing assistant, in addition to which he had taken an operating-room scrub-technicians' course 'down south' some years before.

They waited while Owen rigged up a cloth over a metal screen attached to the operating table so that Mr Q would not be able to see what was being done to his foot. Before coming in, Owen had inserted an intra-venous line in Mr Q's arm, attached to a bag of sterile fluid. Into this line he now injected a sedative drug, to help their patient relax and to control the pain, all the time talking to him calmly in his own language. A reluctant respect for him confused Alanna's feelings still further.

The old man was a diabetic, which was why he now had gangrene in his big toe, a common occurrence because of poor circulation. By doing this operation, they were trying to save the foot, even though such wounds did not heal well. Alanna stood silently watching, admiring the quiet stoicism of the old man. Once he was discharged home, later that day, they would have to 'make periodic house calls to change the dressing for as long as the wound took to heal.

'Now, Alanna.' Her colleague turned his attention to her. 'What would you like to use for a local anaesthetic?'

'I thought I'd use plain Xylocaine, two per cent.'

'Sure.' His eyes smiled at her over the top of his mask. A deceptive charm, she knew that. Then she began to concentrate totally on the job in hand.

'Here we go, Mr Q.' She smiled at Mr Qitdlarssuaq over the top of the drapes as she made a start, thinking he would understand that common local expression that seemed to be applied to many actions.

'OK,' he replied sleepily, barely able to open his eyes.

'You say "swab" and we say "sponge". . .and you say "appendicectomy", while we say 'appendectomy", isn't that right?' Owen queried her, trying to keep the atmosphere light.

'Yes, that is right,' she laughed. 'I. . . I've read about all those different expressions. . .' She had almost given herself away, had almost said that Tim had explained it all to her. She would have to be careful.

It took only a few minutes to amputate the toe, which was black with gangrene. There wasn't much bleeding. Very soon she was neatly and expertly putting in the skin sutures. Owen stood near by watching quietly, saying nothing, while Mr Q snored gently under the influence of the narcotic. Skip helped her while she applied the final dressing, padding and bandage to the foot.

Bonnie Mae returned as they were wheeling Mr Q out of the operating-room, just in time to be with him in the recovery period. 'Hello there!' she said. 'The skidoo's back, if you would like to take it out, Doc.'

'Shall we do that, Alanna, before lunch? What's on this afternoon, Bonnie Mae?'

'Well, now that you two are here, I've booked a whole lot of patients for the afternoon. . .since we've been without a doctor for two weeks. There's the young adults' clinic. . .lots of incipient pneumonia, I should think, as well as all the runny noses. . .then there's the general medical clinic as well. I thought you could do one each, Doc, while I run between the two.'

'Sure. We'll sort it out between us. Alanna, how about that skidoo ride?'

'Yes.' She removed her mask and gown. 'Now would be a good time. I'll just check Mr Q before we leave; I want him to have some anitbiotics.'

'Good idea. I'll meet you outside in about twenty minutes.'

As she later walked over to her room to change into warm outdoor clothing, looking forward to some fresh air, she was thoughtful, gratified that Owen Bentall had not presumed to comment on her surgical technique. Somehow she did not think that he would do so. . .at least, not this time.

He was right; it was hellishly cold on the skidoo. The sleek machine, square at the back and curved to a blunt point at the front, was open to the elements, with only a low windscreen to protect them. The handlebars were like those of a motorbike, and there was a generous-sized seat behind, enough for two people. The whole machine was balanced on two sturdy skis.

'Hang on to me. . .put your arms around my waist . . .grab on to my belt. I'll just go very slowly until you get the feel of it.'

Alanna nodded, clinging firmly to the belt of his snowsuit, glad of her own warm snow-pants, the heavy parka and the boots, mukluks. They were surrounded by a sea of gleaming white snow. Beyond the medical station was the open tundra, mainly flat with only a few gentle undulations. Looking west, the village stretched out before them, with the control tower of the airstrip at the far end. Looking north, not far away, she could see Coronation Gulf and the coastguard ice-breaker moored there.

'Here we go!' The engine roared and Owen manoeuvred the machine carefully away from the buildings, then picked up speed as he steered them towards the expanse of snow. 'We'll go out for a little run. Hold tight!'

In no time at all they were away from the village. After a few moments Alanna rested her hooded cheek against her colleague's broad back to shield herself from the wind, looping her hands through his belt. The ride was exhilarating, like being on the bumper cars at a fairground. She let out a shriek as they went over a particularly high bump and Owen Bentall turned a grinning face towards her. They were picking up speed, two tiny dots of humanity reliant on a machine to keep them safe. Already they were far enough away that walking back, if they had to, would be quite a feat.

Presently Owen slowed the skidoo to a cruising speed, then stopped the engine. 'Like to have a little walk? It might be a bit tough going without snow-shoes.'

'Yes, why not?' She swung herself off the machine, feeling clumsy in the heavy clothing, as though she were doing everything in slow motion. They walked towards the bay, on top of the frozen snow.

'As I was telling you yesterday, we don't normally come out here without a rifle, because of the bears, so we won't stay long. Usually they're as scared as hell of the skidoos and give them a wide berth; they know they mean guns and hunting. Even so, there's no point taking a risk. Later on today I'll show you the guns.'

'Are there a lot of house calls to make here?'

'Quite a lot. The policy is to keep people in their homes unless they are really sick. They prefer it, and their families can look after them. . .there isn't the staff at the clinic to have inpatients for more than a day or two. Going into the homes is good for preventative medicine as well; we can build up a rapport with people so that they want to come to us.'

'What about X-rays?' They were strolling casually away from the skidoo, their crunching footsteps the only sound.

'Skip takes those. . .one of his many talents. He took a radiographers' course for the purpose. One of us has to decide what the pictures mean, since we don't have the luxury of a radiologist.'

They stopped walking to look around them. 'One feels so insignifcant here,' she said. 'As though. . .if there were a battle between man and nature, nature would always win. It's all so impersonal. . .so relentless.'

'Yes, that's true,' he said quietly, 'but after a while here. . .especially if you spend any length of time out on the tundra, or canoeing on the lakes. . .you gradually no longer feel apart from nature, you come to feel at one with it. . . After all, we are a part of it. It's only

our so-called civilisation that has made us feel that
we're above it. . .a natural arrogance of the human
species, I guess. The Inuit and the Indians know all
about that. It takes time.'

'Have I got enough time, do you think? I feel such a
transient.'

He turned to look at her consideringly, squinting
against the sun that held no warmth in it. For a
few moments there seemed to be a strange, silent
communion between them. Alanna knew that she
wanted to feel part of this place, to feel the inner quiet,
to feel the merging of the self with nature. . .even if she
never came here again in her entire life. . .perhaps
especially if she never came here again. . .

'It depends somewhat on a willingness to let go. . .to
go with the flow, so to speak, more than to do with
actual time.' He spoke hesitantly, as though at a loss for
words for once in his life. 'One has to learn the way of
the world up here. . .to respect it. . .in order to know
one's place, in order to survive. Sometimes you know it
intuitively. We're puny compared with the bears, the
eagles, the caribou, the whales. . .all the other animals
and birds that survive here. . .and even more so than
the little flowers that grow right here in the summer,
under our feet.'

'There are whales here? I didn't know that.'

'Yes, they pass through the gulf here in the summer,
migrating north. There are schools of white whales. . .
they're spectacular. . .and some things called narwhals
that have a very long twisted tusk, that look like
something out of a fairy-tale. . .the unicorns of the sea.'

They were strolling back now to their motorised sled.
'You love this place, don't you?'

'Perhaps I do,' he admitted, 'although I think, if I'm
honest, that it's the idea of it more than the actuality

. . .because it's part of my heritage. . .although less so, of course, than for the Inuit and the Indians. A lot of very courageous people live up here; there's also a lot of ignorance, a lack of sophistication. I wasn't joking when I said that I'd rather be in Barbados right now. Coming here once in a while is a sort of renewal.'

'Where are you from?'

'My parents live on Vancouver Island, in the Pacific; I grew up there for the most part. My dad's a general surgeon there. He hopes that one day I'll go back there and take over from him, when I've had my fill of this sort of thing. My mother's a psychologist.'

'It sounds very secure and safe.' And wealthy and privileged too, she thought. 'I've seen pictures of the island. . .it looks very beautiful. . .' Her own background had been less than privileged; her mother had been widowed twice, had struggled in her job as a teacher to keep and educate two children. Money had always been tight.

'Yes, it is,' he said. 'Let's get back. I want to show you the general store, the Royal Canadian Mounted Police headquarters, otherwise known as the RCMP, and a few other places, as well as the homes of some of our patients. I've got a list. Shouldn't take long.'

'Thanks for bringing me out here.'

'Perhaps you'd like to go canoeing some time? Perhaps we could take a long weekend off, take a helicopter or plane a little way south to one of the lakes . . .when the weather's warmer. You'd see some trees and some wildlife. Bonnie Mae could take care of things here.'

'Yes. . . I'd like to do that, very much.'

'That's settled, then. One tends to go stark raving mad without any time off.'

On the way back to the village she felt a renewed

optimism that perhaps he was going to accept her after all. Certainly at the present time he was being very affable. She could quite see how a woman could fall for him. As they drove slowly through the icy lanes between the houses of the village, taking care to avoid other skidoos, she reminded herself again that her relationship with Owen Bentall was strictly professional, that she would not let her guard down until she had found out at least some inside information about the legal inquiry surrounding her brother. Besides, she was an alien in his world, a world of affluence and privilege with which she could not compete.

Later that afternoon, after lunch, the two clinics got going with a vengeance. Bonnie Mae had organised everything very thoroughly and between the three of them they arranged a method of coping with it all, with Alanna starting off in the general medical clinic, Owen in the young adults' clinic. Halfway through the afternoon they made a switch, so that Alanna could have a chance to see what conditions she would have to deal with in the young people who were considered too old to come to the paediatric clinic, but not yet adults. The small waiting-room was full when they started. When anything a bit out of the ordinary occurred, the two doctors would confer with each other.

Towards the end of the afternoon Alanna checked the waiting area twice to make sure that there were no more patients, then when she checked it a third time she saw a young boy sitting there quietly. He had taken off his heavy jacket and boots.

'Hello.' She smiled. 'Are you a patient, or just waiting for someone else?'

'I've come to get a prescription for a Breath-Pac,' he

said matter-of-factly, 'for my asthma. The other one's finished.'

'Oh. . . I've never heard of a Breath-Pac. What is it?' She sat down beside him, noting how thin he looked under the loose clothing, his face more aquiline than the usual round, full features of the Inuit, his warm brown eyes larger.

'It's an inhaler I carry with me in case I get short of breath,' he said quietly, darting her a quick glance, then looking at the floor, as though he could not believe that she had never heard of a Breath-Pac.

'Well, tell me your name; I'll have to get your medical chart out of the files. And how old are you?'

'I'm Tommy Patychuk, and I'm fourteen.'

Alanna hid her surprise well. Judging by his size, she would have guessed that the boy was about ten years old. 'I'm Dr Hargrove. I'll be back in a few minutes, Tommy. I'll want to listen to your chest before I give you a prescription and may get Dr Bentall to have a look at you as well.'

'OK. Can I bring my dog inside, please? She'll be cold out there.'

'Er. . .yes. . . I don't see why not. Is she big?'

'No, she's a pup.' As quick as a flash he was at the door, letting in a flurry of snowflakes as he led in a husky pup who had been tied to the rail on the top step.

'She's absolutely adorable!' Alanna exclaimed in delight. 'Just like a ball of fluff. Can I touch her?' The dog trotted to the centre of the room.

'Yes,' Tommy said proudly. 'She's friendly. I'm training her.'

Alanna knelt down and put her arms around the pup, whose thick layer of springy hair was covered with snowflakes. Strange pale eyes stared out inquisitively from a head made large by fluffy hair, as she reached forward to lick Alanna's cheek.

'She likes you,' Tommy stated. 'She doesn't take to everyone.'

The pup's paws were made large and spatulate by small balls of ice that were attached to the hairs between the toes, giving her a comic, clown-like appearance. Already the ice balls were beginning to melt on the carpet when the pup flopped down to gnaw at them.

'Well, Tommy, this is the first real husky I've ever seen close up like this; I'm really glad you gave me the chance to meet her. Now, you leave her here and come into a cubicle where I can examine you and weigh you.'

'OK.'

Half an hour later Tommy Patychuk departed with his puppy, a prescription in his pocket to take to the local small pharmacy.

'We try to prevent him from getting bronchitis in the winter,' Owen explained to Alanna when he had gone, 'which we were successful in doing this year. He has to be watched all the time. . .for respiratory infections. . . tuberculosis. The Breath-Pac is for emergencies only, if he has trouble breathing. He understand that. Hopefully, he'll outgrow the asthma; there are signs that he might. We just want him to put on some weight. I always give him vitamin tablets to take home when he's here, free of charge. There isn't much money in that family.'

'I see. . .' Alanna said thoughtfully. 'He seems like a sweet boy. . .like his puppy.'

'Yeah, he's a great kid. He's part Indian, part Inuit. His mother was a Cree.'

'Was?' Alanna queried.

'She died when Tommy was six. . .of pneumonia.'

'Oh. . .' She bit her lip in dismay. 'Perhaps that explains why he looks so. . .forlorn.'

'Yeah, maybe. That's a common occurrence up here. Fortunately he's got a large extended family, as well as two sisters. They all love him.' There was a faintly mocking note in his voice, which she did not believe was genuine. Glancing at him swiftly, she was convinced that he was as moved as she was by the plight of the boy who was fourteen and looked ten.

'That's it, Doc,' Bonnie Mae announced, when the last patients, a mother and child, finally left, letting a blast of cold air enter the centrally heated interior of the clinic.

Alanna sat at the desk in the tiny office that had been allocated to her, originally designed as a cupboard, she suspected, to finish her paperwork. She bent over the folder in which she was writing, completing her notes on the last patient, filling in the details of the medical history on the forms to go with the specimens of blood and urine that she had taken. A sense of interest had engaged her attention for the whole afternoon as she had worked, so that she had scarcely been aware of the passage of time.

'How's it going?' Her colleague stood in the doorway later, lounging against the side, his eyes on her face. His dark hair curled almost boyishly around his lean face, softening his features, as though he had run his hands through it many times. Unconsciously her gaze went over him, taking in the muscular shape beneath the scrub suit, noting that he looked tired. It had been a full day for both of them after the long trek that they had made to get there such a short while ago. Already her other life was fast receding.

'Almost finished, just completing my notes.' She smiled back at him. All day she had been aware that he

was watching her, even when they had not been in the
same room, seeming to take note of how long she had
taken to examine a patient, had flipped through some
of her charts later to see what diagnoses she had made,
what treatments and drugs she had prescribed. 'These
are all my charts.' She tapped the pile of folders on her
desk. 'Perhaps you would like to go through them?'

'That won't be necessary.' His eyes flickered with a
recognition of her awareness. 'You did a great job
today.'

'Thank you. Perhaps I could look at your charts
briefly. . . I like to compare notes.'

'Sure.' If he was surprised, he didn't show it. 'All the
specimens we've taken today go in an insulated box
with the completed forms, then Skip takes them down
to the airstrip to go on the next available flight to
Yellowknife. If there's anything really urgent, of
course, I look at it here for a quick diagnosis. . . I've
done some pathology and haematology. . .although I
don't kid myself that mine is the final word. If your
forms are complete, I'll show you where we keep the
box.'

'Yes, they are. . .thanks.' She got to her feet, gathering up the forms. 'I could use a cup of tea!'

'We can call it quits now. This has been what I would
call a typical outpatient day.'

Later she spent fifteen minutes looking through the
charts of his patients before they were filed, noting what
tests he ordered, how often he asked the patients to
come back to see him. The histories were very thorough. Here was a doctor who was obviously very careful
not to let any relevant information slip through without
being recorded.

When she finally returned to their living quarters she
found Owen in the tiny sitting-room watching the news

on television, with a large tray of assorted sandwiches and other paraphernalia for tea on the small table in front of him. 'I thought you'd deserted me,' he murmured, looking up at her as she came hesitantly into the room as though she were invading his privacy. 'Come in. Have some tea before I consume it all.'

'Thanks. I'm ravenous.'

When she had filled a plate with food, she turned her attention to the television screen, not really seeing the moving shapes there. Living with Owen Bentall might not be as straightforward as her blithe earlier assumptions had led her to believe. In Birmingham she would have gone out with friends after work when she was not on call, to a restaurant, a pub, to a film or a concert. Here there was literally nowhere to go, except out for a walk on the tundra, carrying a rifle, or for a skidoo ride. Occasionally there was a dance in the local church hall, so she had heard, and there was a bar of sorts. In between times one had to be inventive, create one's own entertainment and diversion when work was over.

'There's a medical condition here called "cabin fever",' he said, as though reading her thoughts. 'It's an officially recognised phenomenon. . .a psychological syndrome that people get when they're confined in a particular place for a long time. . .because of bad weather, for instance. Another name for it is "stir crazy"; prisoners get it.'

'I've heard of it. Are you hinting that we're going to be stricken?'

He stretched out his long legs in front of him, put his hands comfortably behind his head. 'Just something to watch out for,' he said. She couldn't tell how serious he was. 'We have to make sure we get some relaxation and variety in our lives.'

As though to call his bluff, the intercom telephone in

his room buzzed loudly, making Alanna jump. Silently he got up and went out to the narrow passage from which their rooms led off. They were effectively on call twenty-four hours a day, even though they could later work out a schedule for taking turns getting up in the first instance at night. Bonnie Mae was the one who was under the most stress, being the first line of defence.

Presently he came back in. 'There's an acute abdomen over there,' he said calmly. 'Bonnie Mae thinks something's perforated, so they're getting the operating-room ready. No, you stay here.' He put a warm hand on her shoulder, pressing her down as she made a movement to get up. 'Finish your tea; eat as much as you can in case we don't get any supper. I'll take a look, then I'll call you.' He put on the white lab coat that he had flung carelessly over a chair, then was quickly gone, leaving her sitting there holding a teacup, feeling a little superfluous.

Perhaps he had intended her to feel that way, to let her know that he was very much in charge, not letting her have a chance to make a diagnosis herself. She could compromise — eat her tea then go over there without waiting to be called. At the moment she had to rely very much on him. Only her good training and experience gave her confidence in this unknown place.

The intercom telephone in her room buzzed before she had done more than eat a few sandwiches and change into a clean scrub suit. 'We'll have to do a laparotomy,' Owen said abruptly at the other end of the line. 'It looks like a perforated gut, possibly a ruptured diverticulum. Can you give the anaesthetic?'

'Yes. I'll come over straight away. I'd like time to do a cross-match.'

'Sure. Bonnie Mae's setting it up right now.'

As she hurried through the covered walkway towards

the operating-room, her wool coat over her scrub suit, she had a sense that everything was moving much too quickly. Owen had not even had time to show her the rifles yet as he had promised.

CHAPTER FOUR

'I GOT out three units of blood, Dr Hargrove,' Bonnie Mae called to Alanna as soon as she made an appearance in the operating-room. 'Will that be enough? And Dr Bentall took a blood sample from the patient. It's there waiting for you in the lab.' For all her bulk, Bonnie Mae moved with amazing alacrity as she and Skip prepared the operating-room for the case. 'Doc's with the patient; he's putting in the IV and getting a stomach tube down.'

'Good. I probably won't need any blood at all, but I want to have it ready just in case.'

'Sure. We'll be ready when you are.'

Alanna put on a pair of cotton overshoes and a face mask and cap in preparation for the operation. She hurried into the small lab to set up the blood samples for the cross-match; that was her first priority, since her colleague was dealing with the patient. As she worked she found that her heart was beating fast, and she chided herself for wanting to be especially efficient to impress Owen.

In the operating-room she checked the anaesthetic machine, to make sure that all the gases and the drugs she would need were on hand, including several bags of intravenous fluid. No doubt the patient would be dehydrated.

'How soon can we make a start?' Owen Bentall had come in silently, to stand near her. 'I've started the IV. . . Ringer's lactate. . .is that OK with you?'

'Yes. I'm more or less ready here. I'd like to examine

the patient, of course, and I'd like to have the blood ready first if possible; but if we can't wait for that we'll make a start.'

'I'd rather get on with it. There's really no need for you to examine the patient. . . I've given him a very thorough going over. . .a forty-five-year-old man, doesn't smoke, doesn't drink much, not overweight; he's in pretty good shape apart from the perforation. Blood-pressure OK, et cetera.'

'All the same, I never give an anaesthetic without examining the patient first, unless he happens to be bleeding to death,' she replied calmly.

Alanna heard him draw in a breath sharply behind his mask, as though he would say something to contradict her. She felt that he was pulling rank on her, as well as testing her, so without another word she took her stethoscope and left the room, leaving Skip preparing his instruments and sutures. The patient, a man from down south who worked at the harbour, was very pale, almost grey, obviously in a lot of pain which he was tolerating stoically.

'Hello, Mr Racine,' she said, picking up the chart to read his name and the diagnosis that had been made. 'I'm Dr Hargrove, I'll be giving you your anaesthetic. Before we make a start I'd just like to listen to your chest. Have you had a general anaesthetic before?'

'No. . .never. Never been really sick in my life, apart from a bit of indigestion now and then.' Mr Racine spoke with difficulty, gritting his teeth against the pain.

'I'll be as quick as I can, then we can do something about the pain.' Under the watchful and obviously impatient regard of her colleague, who had followed her out, Alanna listened to his chest with her stethoscope and asked him some pertinent questions about the state of his heart and lungs.

'Your chest sounds clear,' she said. 'Everything should be very straightforward.' She smiled to reassure him, doing everything in a calm, unhurried fashion. There was no way that she was going to compromise her standards. She helped Bonnie Mae to wheel Mr Racine into the operating-room, then to position him on the operating table.

'If you're all ready, Bonnie,' Owen Bentall asked from the doorway, 'I'll get scrubbed.'

'Sure, you get scrubbed, Doc, but don't rush,' Bonnie Mae replied succinctly. 'Skip and I have to do the sponge and instrument count before you can make a start. And I want to help Dr Hargrove first.'

Alanna smiled to herself as she drew up the anaesthetic drugs in the syringes. He was a typical surgeon, impatient to scrub and start cutting. There were no flies on Bonnie Mae; she knew how to handle him, well aware that this was an emergency and they did have to move quickly. She adjusted an oxygen mask over the patient's nose and mouth.

'Take a few breaths of oxygen, Mr Racine.'

'Give 'em an inch and they take ten miles.' The nurse grinned at her, as though reading her thoughts. 'Those surgeons are all the same, don't matter where you are. If you don't keep 'em firmly in hand they tramp all over you.' She said it in a jocular manner for the benefit of the listening patient, giving him a wink as she said it. Skip and Alanna knew that she was deadly serious.

Alanna injected the Pentothal into the patient's intravenous line and in seconds he was unconscious without knowing what had hit him. 'Pass me the laryngoscope please, Bonnie, then that number 7.5 endotracheal tube. I certainly admire your aplomb with Dr Bentall; I've been admiring it ever since I got here. You'll have to give me a few lessons.'

'Gee, if you think I've got aplomb, that makes my day!' She passed the 'scope, then held the tube ready. 'You just don't let them get on top of you—if you'll excuse the pun—otherwise they can make your life hell. Right, Skip?'

'Right!' Skip, silent up to then, grinned at them conspiratorially over his mask. 'I've met my fair share of bad-tempered surgeons.'

Bonnie handed Alanna the endotracheal tube and she expertly inserted it. 'Thank you, Bonnie. Could you switch on the monitor and connect the pulse oxymeter, please? Then I can manage, if you want to get on with your sponge count. . .and I'll need the blood warmer later.'

'Sure. Come on, Skip, let's do the count before we have Doc breathing down our necks.'

Half an hour later Owen Bentall was still bending over the abdominal incision, searching carefully for perforations. Although his diagnosis had been right, it had become clear fairly early on that there was more than one perforation in the colon and that he would not be able to do a simple repair job. 'I'm going to have to do a partial colectomy, Dr Hargrove,' he had said. 'I'll get on with it as soon as I can be absolutely sure that I know where all the perforations are. Is that OK with you? How's the patient doing?'

'Oh, he's all right. You do whatever you have to do. I've got the blood on hand; there's no problem from my end.' The truth was, she was feeling a little nervous, hoping fervently that they would not get into any major bleeding. Most of the anaesthetics she had given in the past had been for fairly short operations. She knew that she and Owen would have to take turns in staying up all night with Mr Racine.

At last it was over. The partial colectomy was done, a drainage tube put into the patient's abdomen and connected to an electric suction pump, the incision sutured closed. Alanna had watched, mostly in silence, as Owen had worked, assisted by Skip who had practically tied himself in knots playing the dual roles of scrub nurse and surgical assistant, while Bonnie Mae had been the 'circulating' nurse. There was no doubt that Owen was a very good surgeon, working calmly and carefully, obviously knowing exactly what he had to do, then doing it without hesitation.

They stood around Mr Racine in the small recovery-room off the main operating-room, waiting for him to recover from the anaesthetic. He would remain connected to a monitor for the rest of the night, which automatically showed his heart-rate and graph, his blood-pressure and temperature, as well as the amount of circulating oxygen in his bloodstream. Alanna had needed to use only one unit of blood during the operation.

'Shall I take the first shift?' she offered. 'I'm too wide awake to sleep, anyway.' She addressed her remark to Owen who stood on the other side of the narrow stretcher on which the patient lay. He looked tired and serious. His eyes met hers consideringly.

'Yes, we don't both need to be here. He seems quite stable now.' His eyes flicked over the monitor again. 'Then you might as well take the morning off to sleep.' He turned to the nurse. 'You stay here as well for about an hour, Bonnie, then you had better get some sleep too. Watch the pump, let me know if there's any bleeding, continue the IV antibiotics. . . I've written it up on the chart, as well as Demerol for pain. And listen for bowel sounds later.'

Then to Alanna's surprise he put his arms round

Bonnie Mae and gave her a quick hug. 'Thanks, Bonnie, you were great, as always.' A presentiment told her that he was going to do the same to her and she steeled herself, holding her breath as he came round to her side of the stretcher.

'Thank you too, Alanna; that was a good anaesthetic.' Quickly he pulled her to him, holding her strongly for a few seconds against his firm, muscular body so that she could feel his warmth through their thin scrub suits. Involuntarily she put her hands up to grasp his arms, while he planted a kiss on the side of her face above the mask that she still wore. For an unguarded moment she wanted to let herself sway forward into the circle of his arms, to put her head against his shoulder, to be held by him. 'Call me if there's a problem. OK?'

'Yes. . .yes, I will.' In the few seconds that their eyes met she read an unmistakable warmth of sexual desire in his, mixed with something else. . .a certain awareness that he was boss. A mischievous urge compelled her to add, 'You were pretty good yourself, Dr Bentall!'

She resented the assumption that he alone had the right to confer blessings on others, even though his unexpected gesture seemed entirely spontaneous and was oddly touching as they stood around the sick man, all still very keyed-up and aware that the battle for his well-being was far from over. Indeed, she felt an emotional constriction of her throat and a pricking of tears in her eyes as she looked at Edouard Racine's wan face, a familiar compassion that always translated into the desire to do something.

'Sweet of you to say so, Dr Hargrove,' Owen murmured, letting her go. 'As you know, surgeons have big egos. . .they probably wouldn't be able to operate otherwise, in any sense of the word. . .but it's still nice to hear someone say you did a good job. One doesn't get too many accolades up here.'

Did you offer any to my brother? The thought came sharply to her mind.

'Well. . .goodnight. Don't hesitate to call if you're worried about anything.' He strode quickly to the door and was gone.

'Phew! I'm glad that's over.' Bonnie Mae articulated the relief that they both felt. 'I think I've got enough adrenalin coursing through my body to keep six people going for a week.'

Alanna laughed, feeling herself relax. The monitor hummed, spewing out a cardiograph. She checked the intravenous line to make sure that the fluid was still running into the patient's vein and not into the tissue of his arm.

'I'll make us a drink and a sandwich, Dr Hargrove. Tea or coffee?'

'I'd better have tea, otherwise I won't be able to sleep later. . .please. Does Dr Bentall always hug his colleagues after an operation?'

'Only when he's really relieved about something, or he thinks we did especially well. He's a great guy really, even though we moan about him sometimes. He's one of the best.'

'Perhaps he was relieved because he expected me to screw up,' Alanna ventured. 'He didn't want a woman doctor here, you know. He told me as much.'

The nurse looked enigmatic. 'You were great,' she said. 'It didn't take us long to realise that you're going to be worth your salt. If he seems anti-woman, maybe he has reason to be. He had his fiancée up here working with him once. . .she was a real disaster. I could tell you about that if I had about two days to spare. What a lulu she was!'

'A fiancée? I. . . I didn't know he had one.'

'Probably hasn't now. . .he hasn't said a word about her. And he sure ain't married. She was a real glamour-puss, totally unsuited to being up here; she seemed to think that all she had to do was walk around the place in a white coat with a stethoscope slung around her neck and someone else would do all the work. She only stayed for three weeks. Geez! The memory of it makes me wanna puke.' With that parting remark she left the room.

'Thank God for modern technology.' Alanna smiled at Bonnie Mae later as they sipped their tea at one end of the small room while the monitor recorded the vital signs of their patient. Alarm bells would ring if the slightest irregularity occurred in his condition. 'This is the nicest cup of tea I've had for some time. What's going to happen tomorrow with staffing this place? We've all got to get some sleep.'

'Skip can take care of outpatients and minor emer-gencies. I can call in a nursing aide from the village if I have to. There are no clinics tomorrow, so we're in luck. The three of us will just have to take turns with Mr Racine here round the clock until he's well enough to go home. In the old days he would have been shipped out of here pretty quick. This is the best way. Some didn't make it.'

'Actually, Bonnie, if you've got all your notes up to date, you might as well go off to sleep now. I can manage here till morning, if you can just show me where I can find a few things.'

'OK. . .then I'll be bright and breezy first thing in the morning.'

The telephone buzzed in the recovery-room later, causing Alanna's head to jerk up. She had dozed off for a few seconds in the quiet room, where the only sounds were the patient's steady breathing and the low hum of the monitor, interspersed with the occasional distant sound of wind gusting outside.

'Hello.' Very quickly she was fully alert.

'How's it going, Alanna?' Owen's deep voice held a concerned note that seemed to empathise with her long, lonely vigil.

'Everything's all right so far,' she answered, *sotto voce*. 'Mr Racine's asleep again, not in any pain at the moment. His condition's stable, the pump's going still . . .a little blood-stained fluid. . .mostly clear.' She inhaled a large breath, forcing herself to think clearly, to go over everything, not wanting to leave anything out by which he could later have reason to judge her negatively. Their concern now was to clear up the underlying peritonitis with antibiotics. 'I'm aspirating him regularly via the stomach tube.'

'What IV fluids are you giving him?' When he had quizzed her on several more points, he informed her that he was coming over to relieve her. Looking at her watch, she saw that it was a quarter to five o'clock. . . the beginning of her fourth day in Chalmers Bay. Had she really only arrived there on Monday? Already it seemed so much longer. Now that relief was at hand she was aware of being utterly exhausted.

'Coffee for you!' Owen had come in silently while she had been bending over the chart at the desk. When she turned he was standing there with a mug of coffee in his hand, its tantalising aroma filling the room. Obviously he had just taken a shower, his wet hair sleeked back from his lean face. Unlike her, he looked fresh and well-rested.

'Mm. . .that smells wonderful. I'll risk not being able to sleep with all that caffeine in my body. Thank you.'

'I've cooked breakfast for you as well, a huge one, since I'm sure you'll need it. . .grilled bacon and pancakes.'

'Pancakes! For breakfast!' She felt suddenly shy, confronted again by this very attractive man who had cooked breakfast for her.

'Sure. You eat them with a little butter and some maple syrup; there's a pile for you in the oven.'

'I appreciate that. . .thank you. I haven't known any men who knew how to cook pancakes.'

Taking the patient's chart from her, he began to flip slowly through it. 'I have to confess,' he smiled, 'that I made them from Aunt Jemima's Pancake Mix. . .we buy it along at the store.'

'Really?' She laughed.

'Sure. You just add eggs and milk. Now, Alanna. . .' he put a casual arm around her shoulders '. . .if there's nothing else that you have to tell me, you go to bed, take the rest of the day off. There isn't much doing. I'll only call you if there's some sort of emergency.'

'Oh, I couldn't do that. . . I can get up in the afternoon. After all, I did come here to work.'

'Yes, but not to overwork; you have sort of had a baptism by fire, so to speak. Just sleep for a while, then relax. . . I'll see you later, for tea, or supper. OK?'

'All right,' she reluctantly agreed, 'but please don't let me sleep if there are things to do. . .' The words of Bonnie Mae came back to her, describing his fiancée as useless. 'I wouldn't feel happy about that.' The thought of him with a fiancée put everything in a wholly new light.

'I know you wouldn't,' he agreed gently. 'Not to worry. . . I'll be the first to wake you. Now, about the weekend. . .you have a choice to be off for the

Saturday or Sunday. Think about it. Now, go get those pancakes.'

'Thanks. . . Owen.' Quickly she left the room.

The hot pancakes with the maple syrup were delicious, satisfying and filling. She made a mental note to buy herself some Aunt Jemima's Pancake Mix when she explored the village grocery store. In her room the bed looked so inviting that she could have flung herself down on it and fallen instantly asleep. As it was, she forced herself to have a shower and wash her hair. Then under the warm duvet, with only a few fleeting pangs of homesickness beforehand, she drifted into oblivion.

The sound of a door opening or closing woke her. When her eyelids flickered open she saw someone standing in her room, indistinct in the dim light. The somnolence of sleep gave way to a momentary alarm before he spoke.

'It's me. . . Owen.' His voice was low and deep. Alanna had the odd feeling that he had been standing there for some time, watching her.

'Is. . .is something happening?' She felt disorientated.

'No. . .nothing. Sorry to wake you.' He sat down on the edge of her bed as though he needed to rest. 'I just intended to leave a note on your bedside table to let you know what I'm doing.' He seemed to take it for granted that he could come into her room.

She sat up quickly, the movement bringing his face close to her own. Without making it obvious, she hoped, that his nearness disturbed her greatly, she slowly drew back, propping herself up on her arms. At the same time she was uncomfortably aware that this position brought her breasts into prominence against the thin material of her nightdress and that the movement had diverted his attention from her face to her body. As he looked at her his eyes darkened with a heightened appreciation, so that when he again raised his eyes to meet hers the sexual invitation in them was unmistakable.

Earlier in the night she had wanted him to hold her, to comfort her. . . Now, overwhelmingly, she wanted it in a different way. The tightness in her throat made it impossible for her to speak; she could only stare at him. Again she felt that he was testing her in some way. Perhaps the reservations that he had expressed to her when they had first met were becoming a self-fulfilling prophecy. None of the other young men she had shared living quarters with in the past had disturbed her equanimity like this. She had breezed through their tenancy in her life like a scarcely awakened Sleeping Beauty. In contrast, Owen Bentall was very adult and very male.

'I wanted to let you know myself that I'm going out for a walk. . . I badly need some fresh air. I'm going to take one of the guns and walk east. . .not too far. That's where I'll be if you need to come looking for me. Everything's fine over at the clinic; there's no need for you to get up. Bonnie Mae will give you a buzz if there's anything doing, and Skip can come after me in the skidoo if necessary. OK?'

'Yes.' She found her voice. 'How's Mr Racine?'

'He's fine. . .awake and alert. . .talking, even cracking a few jokes. We'll keep him on the antibiotics for at least ten days, and the IV fluids for a while longer.'

'Um. . .perhaps you would show me how the rifle works before you go out. I might decide to go for a walk myself.' Anything to get him out of the room.

When he had left she scrambled out of bed quickly and put on a robe and slippers, going out into the sitting-room so that he did not have a reason to invade her private room again. Sunshine streamed in through the window. Even so, a few thin flakes of snow were floating gently down.

'It seems so incongruous,' she said, 'to see sunshine and snow at the same time. In England it's usually grey and dull when it's snowing.'

'Yes. . .one of the many things that you have to get used to,' he said levelly, making her feel that he was talking about more than the weather and other routine things. 'Here's your gun. You put in the ammunition . . .like so. . .and you carry more in your pocket. This is the safety catch. Make sure it's on. Carry the rifle with you at all times. . .don't leave it on a skidoo or in a tent. You never know where or when you might meet a bear. The polar bears hunt, kill and eat people. A bit further south there are grizzlies. They can kill you with one swipe of a paw, if they have a mind to do so.'

Alanna shivered, contemplating an unexpected encounter with a huge grizzly. 'I'll remember,' she said. There were two rifles in the cupboard and a box of ammunition. The key was hidden in the kitchen.

'While I'm at it,' he added matter-of-factly, 'I might as well show you how to put on the snow-shoes. A lot of the time you don't need them here because the snow's generally frozen solid under the fresh layer, but sometimes you come across a patch where you sink down in it if you're wearing ordinary boots. We keep a few pairs here.' From another cupboard he took out a pair of snow-shoes, looking like old, elongated tennis rackets, but with wider leather mesh thongs between the wooden frames.

She watched carefully while he showed her how to lace them on to boots. 'It takes a while to get the hang of walking in a pair of these,' he informed her casually.

She didn't doubt it. There was so much to learn 'up North'.

When he was finally gone she cooked herself lunch from the basic supplies they had in the refrigerator, planning what she would do for the rest of the day. In spite of what Owen had said, that there was nothing doing at the clinic, she would go over there to see Mr Racine and offer to help Bonnie Mae. Then, if there really was nothing doing, she would take the other rifle and walk too. It would be good to get out.

CHAPTER FIVE

THE sun sparkled on new snow as she walked east, away from the village. Wind ruffled the wolf fur on the hood of her parka, making a faint whistling noise as it scudded around her well-padded figure. In the snow-pants, heavy parka and mukluks, she felt herself moving in slow motion, the trousers making a swishing sound as the nylon coverings rubbed together. Over her back, on a long strap, she had slung the snow-shoes, while in her right hand she carried the rifle.

As she walked away from Chalmers Bay the sounds of the village grew fainter — the occasional whine of a skidoo, the blast of a ship's siren, and the roar of a Cessna taking off from the airstrip. Strange though everything was, especially the feel of the rifle, heavy in her hand, she was beginning to feel, tentatively, a part of this place. She had a job to do; she could be useful here.

As she walked on into the singing wind, her boots crunching in the frozen snow, she felt a peace descending on her as though she were entering a vast, silent cathedral where a spiritual presence overwhelmed the petty everyday concerns of humans, putting all in perspective. With her sunglasses on against the glare she searched the horizon for Owen Bentall, admitting to herself that she had come this way in hopes of meeting him. Perhaps later on she would be avoiding him, like the proverbial plague, she thought ruefully, when they had been working together and living together for several weeks. There was no sign of him.

76

She had been walking for twenty minutes, glancing back every so often to see how far she was from the outskirts of the village and the reassuring low buildings of the medical station. It would not be wise to lose sight of the buildings entirely; it would be very easy to become disorientated in an expanse of snow with no visible landmarks.

Then she saw a dark shape a few hundred yards ahead of her and recognised Owen's black snowsuit. He appeared to be kneeling, as though looking at someting in the snow. The faint apprehension that she had felt at being alone on the open tundra was dissipated at the sight of him. Whatever else he was, he inspired trust. Pushing back the enveloping hood from her face, she shouted at him, 'Owen! Owen!' He did not look up.

A movement over to her right registered on the periphery of her vision and, turning her head slowly towards it, she felt a thrill of absolute terror as she saw a polar bear moving at speed in what seemed like a direct line towards Owen. It was difficult to tell exactly how fast it was moving until she had both the man and the animal in her line of vision, then it was frighteningly obvious that the gap between them was closing fast. Owen had his back to the animal, facing towards the gulf.

'Owen. . .a bear! Bear!' Cupping her hands either side of her mouth, she shouted a warning as loudly as she could, with a voice that was high-pitched with fear. The wind, as though mocking her efforts, seemed to snatch the puny sound away from her with an unseen hand.

It was no good. He very obviously could not hear her. The parka hood that he wore helped to muffle any sound. Alanna began to run, clumsily over the snow, shouting Owen's name as she ran. Already the bear was close enough that she could see the ripples in its thick, cream-coloured coat as it moved. Although a somewhat ungainly creature, it nevertheless had a grace of its own as it moved confidently over the frozen land that was its natural habitat, with a swift, lumbering gallop that brought it closer to the man. It paid no attention whatsoever to her.

Sobbing now with breathlessness and fear, Alanna stopped running, pulled off her gloves and knelt down in the snow. Clumsy in her haste, she removed the safety catch from the rifle, punched a hole in the snow as a place to rest the butt, then, pointing it at the sky, holding it at an angle, she pulled the trigger. The retort was as satisfyingly loud as she had hoped. Then she was on her feet again, shouting, waving and pointing in the direction of the bear, which was, she estimated, less than two hundred metres away from the man.

With awful slowness the kneeling man turned to her, then to look behind him as she gesticulated wildly. Alanna watched, her chest heaving, while he picked up his own rifle and got to his feet. The bear had slowed but not stopped. While she fumbled in her pocket for more ammunition, thinking that the bear could possibly veer in her direction, she saw Owen lift the rifle into the air and fire. This time the lumbering creature made a turn to the east, scarcely faltering in its stride, picking up speed as it now ran from them.

She fell twice trying to reach him. When they finally came together her breath was coming in sobbing rasps. To her he looked much more cool than she felt.

'You OK?' he asked, moving to support her as she swayed against him. 'Here. . .sit down to get your breath back. That was a close call.'

Sitting down on the snow, with her knees drawn up and head bent forward, she fought for breath, drawing the icy air deep into her lungs. Running over rough terrain in a padded suit, carrying snow-shoes and a rifle, was not like anything she had experienced before. Owen sat down beside her, putting a hand on her shoulder. 'I guess I owe you a big thank-you,' he said soberly. 'You probably saved my life. . .or at least saved me from some sort of injury. You can't tell what those bears will do.'

'My God, I was *so* scared. . .it seemed to be running straight at you. I don't know whether that was an optical illusion, it's difficult to tell out here. . .'

'It was coming at me; I'm glad you had the presence of mind to fire the gun. . .' They sat close together, their faces almost touching, as they slowly recovered from the experience. 'Look at that bear now!' He pointed to a rapidly diminishing speck running towards the horizon. 'He won't stop going for miles now. They're as scared as hell of guns.' When he turned back to her, the fur on his parka brushed softly against her cheek. Casually he pushed his hood back, revealing his thick, tousled hair. From this close Alanna could see the lines of tiredness on his face, could study the shape of his mouth, masculine and sensual. . . This time she did not draw back.

'You were very brave,' he said quietly. With his North American drawl the compliment sounded like a line from an old Hollywood movie. She told him so, wanting to lighten the shock.

'If I were John Wayne,' he said, 'the next move would go something like this. . .' Slowly he moved his hand from her shoulder to the back of her head, twining his fingers in her hair, while she found herself holding her breath, waiting. His gaze held hers for a few seconds, then moved to her mouth. Please kiss me. . . The words sounded in her brain as though she had spoken them aloud, vying simultaneously with other words of warning.

When his lips touched hers she closed her eyes, feeling the barely warm northern sun on her lids and the wind ruffling her hair. His hand pulled her closely to him as the kiss deepened, and her arms moved up to encircle his neck. His mouth on hers was firm and confident, yet tender, seeking a sensual response from her that she found herself giving readily, wanting it to go on forever. She nestled against him, as though to reassure herself that he was alive, allowing a few thoughts to enter her mind of what might have happened if he had been killed and she had been left alone with the bear.

When he lifted his mouth from hers she still clung to him, feeling weak with a strange longing. There was a surreal air to everything, alone as they were in this white desert gleaming in the sunlight, with the moaning, whispering wind sending little eddies of soft snow around their bodies. If they stayed for much longer they would be completely covered.

Pushing her back gently against the snow, he leaned over her. 'That was a fair imitation of a Hollywood heroine you did there.' His slow smile warmed his eyes as he looked down on her. 'Perhaps I should warn you that I saw a fair number of old movies when I was a kid . . .especially the westerns where the man always got his woman.'

'For what it's worth, so did I. It's all wrong, somehow . . .no stage-coaches! I might have had to kill that bear.' Alanna tried to keep her tone light, yet heard her voice tremble with emotion. 'Anyway, I thought it was the woman who always got the man.'

'Whatever. . .' he touched her lips lightly with his,

smiling '. . .don't let this experience put you off being here.'

'No? That would be a perfect excuse for you to get rid of me. . .get a man here instead. That's what you want, isn't it?'

'Not any more. You're too handy with a gun, as well as a scalpel. Besides, I like what I'm doing now too much. . .' He kissed her again then, moving his mouth on hers as though he could will her to forget all about the bear. Everything but the feel of him was blotted out as an unaccustomed passion mounted in her and she returned his kisses with a fervour that matched their wild surroundings.

The low buzz of a skidoo engine, like a distant angry wasp, penetrated their consciousness and caused Owen Bentall to sit up. Alanna followed suit more slowly, feeling the cold now penetrating even her insulated clothing. Coming towards them at speed, still a fair way off, was a skidoo. Judging by the shape of the man on it, he was not Skip. They both got up and waved to him, even though there was no doubt that he was coming over to them.

'It's one of the RCMP guys,' Owen commented. 'Must have heard the shots.'

'A Mountie always gets his man. Isn't that their motto?'

'Yeah. . .supposed to be.'

'Let's hope that a Mountie also gets his bear,' she tried to joke, still feeling a little tremulous.

'He'll get the ranger to do that. . .to maybe track it down. Some of those bears are tagged.'

The RCMP officer brought the skidoo around them in a wide dramatic sweep, so that he was facing back towards the village, before he came to a halt. Alanna had almost expected him to be wearing the traditional scarlet jacket, the breeches and the curiously shaped felt hat. Instead, he wore a very prosaic dark blue snowsuit and very sensible heavy black mukluks. He swung himself off his machine, looking them over curiously as he did so.

'Hi there! Someone heard the shots and reported it to us.' He walked over to them, a huge man, over six feet tall. Alanna estimated that he must weigh over three hundred and fifty pounds. The North seemed to attract big, muscular, beefy men. 'Are you folks OK?'

'Yes, we are now, thanks, Greg. We had a hairy few minutes when a bear tried to creep up on me. My colleague here, Dr Hargrove, managed to save the day by firing the gun. We didn't hit it.'

The officer had fair hair and warm brown eyes that were alight with interest as he looked at Alanna, then back to Owen Bentall. 'Dr Bentall, isn't it. . . Owen? I thought you'd left here for the summer.'

'Yes. . . I thought I'd left too. Had to come back in a hurry to help out.'

'I see. Greg Farley, ma'am, RCMP. Glad to meet you.' He held out a hand to Alanna, first removing the gauntlets that he wore. 'Pity you had to meet up with a bear. Which way was that bear heading when you last saw it?' The laconic drawal reminded Alanna once again of John Wayne, giving her the odd feeling that she was really participating in an old movie, until she caught sight of the gleaming skidoo parked incongruously on the snow where there should have been a team of dogs.

Owen Bentall answered for her. 'It was going due east.'

'I'll get the ranger to make sure it stays due east. I sure am glad you folks are OK. By the way you were bending over her, Dr Bentall, I could have sworn you were giving her mouth-to-mouth resuscitation. I thought I'd better get over here pretty quick.'

Owen gave a shout of laughter. 'Your eyes were deceiving you, Greg,' he said, grinning very broadly, while Alanna smiled and said nothing. 'We were just trying to get our breath back.'

'You could have fooled me! Anyway, Doc, I'll just take the lady back on the skidoo here, then I'll come back for you. OK? Give me the rifle, ma'am; I'll just put it out of harm's way on the skidoo.'

'Sure. Thanks, Greg. I'll start walking. See you back at the annexe, Alanna. I'll leave you with the knight in shining armour.'

'It's great to see a pretty southern woman around here,' the RCMP officer commented. 'Not that Bonnie Mae isn't pretty. . .it's just that she tends to make the skidoo break down whenever I take her out. Besides, she's got a boyfriend. . .Chuck, his name is. I wouldn't want to tangle with him. No, sir! You should see the size of him! A real big guy, that one.'

Alanna laughed delightedly, as no doubt he intended that she should, thoughts of the bear beginning to recede from her mind. What did a few bears matter when there were people like Greg Farley around. . .not to mention Owen Bentall? 'Come on, then, ma'am, sling a leg over,' he chivvied her good-humouredly. 'If we don't get going, Dr Bentall will be there ahead of us. That wouldn't look good for the rescue operation now, would it? You hang on to me.'

In a few minutes they were zooming past her colleage, who was walking in a straight line towards the medical station. She grimaced at him as they went by, indicating her alarm at the speed they were going. She supposed it didn't occur to Greg Farley that she might have only been on a skidoo once before. In no time they had come to a halt again outside her living quarters.

'Here's your gun, ma'am. Don't let that experience put you off going out. We'll get the ranger to track down that bear. They tranquillise the bears with a tranquilliser gun, the ones that come back to the community persistently, causing trouble. Then they put them in a net, sling them under a helicopter and take them a long way from here and release them.'

'I'm glad they don't get shot,' Alanna said, with feeling.

'No, we try to conserve our wildlife as much as possible. Now you take care, ma'am; get inside and warm up. I'm going back for the other guy. Bye for now. Hope to see you around.'

'Goodbye. . .and thank you again.'

By the time she got to her room she was shivering from cold and perhaps from delayed shock as well. With shaking hands, teeth chattering, she stripped off her layers of clothing and got under the shower. She was revelling in the sheer joy of the hot water on her skin when she heard the skidoo stop again outside, then the slam of the outer door as her colleague entered the building. With a sense of relief, she turned her attention again to soaping her chilled body.

There was a knock on her bedroom door when she had finished dressing again in a shirt, warm sweater, jeans and heavy socks. 'Come in!'

'I've made us each a mug of hot chocolate; it's in the sitting-room. Then we ought to order our supper from the kitchen. . .give them plenty of notice. Those guys cook for other outfits as well.' Owen stood in the doorway, showered and changed.

'Yes. . .thanks. Just what I need. I'm still in a state

of shock, I think.' She went out to join him. 'I want to go over to the clinic soon to check on Mr Racine, if. . . if that's all right with you.' It was possible that he thought of Mr Racine as his patient and did not want her to interfere now that the immediate crisis was over with him. After all, she had only given the anaesthetic. 'I — um — I assume you would like us to take turns. . .' She found herself stammering a bit, self-consciously, very mindful, now that they were back to safety, that they had been lying in each other's arms a short while ago, kissing passionately. How soon his implied predictions had come true! She found that she could scarcely meet his eyes as she sat in the sitting-room drinking the hot chocolate.

'Yes, of course,' he said curtly, seeming a little annoyed by her hesitation. 'I thought that was what we had decided yesterday. See him by all means. I'm going to get some sleep until suppertime, then I'll take the night call this time. We should make up a roster soon for night calls and weekends.' He seemed restless, moving to stare out of the window as he drank, in another chameleon-like change of mood.

'Yes,' she said, feeling herself acting unnaturally, like someone in a dated play, and irritated with herself for doing so. 'Perhaps we could do it later this evening. . . if there's time.'

'Look. . . I want to apologise for what happened out there.' He turned round abruptly, his face brooding and serious. 'I shouldn't have touched you. . .shouldn't have kissed you the way I did. . .especially after that spiel I gave you on the plane coming up here. You must have thought me a pompous idiot. Then I go ahead and make it happen. . .on the fourth day!'

Wide-eyed, she looked at him. 'It's all right; I. . . I

wanted you to kiss me. For a few minutes out there I was terrified.'

'I know you were. And I took advantage of it. I shouldn't have.' His face looked grim, as though he was angry both with her and with himself.

'But it doesn't matter,' she insisted. 'I needed that. . . I'm not sorry it happened. I was just as responsible as you were.' She stood up to face him. 'You must have been scared as well. To borrow a North American phrase, it's no big deal.'

'It could interfere with our work here. . .'

'Now you are being pompous. Yes, it could, I agree, but we don't have to let it,' she said, assuming that the awkwardness she now felt would soon blow over. This sudden, rather dramatic change of mood in him was alarming, especially when she had begun to feel that she was really getting to know him and like him. It was as though he intended to shut a door very firmly in her face.

'Easier said than done. Please accept my apology. You were great out there. If it hadn't been for your presence of mind. . .if you had decided not to bring the gun after all. . . I hate to think of the consequences.'

'I accept it, but I don't understand. You hugged me in the recovery-room last night, you hugged Bonnie Mae. . . It doesn't mean more than what it seemed.'

'Don't make assumptions on my behalf. That was different.'

She leaned forward earnestly. 'We've built up a good working relationship in a very short time,' she said. 'I don't want anything to interfere with that.'

'That remark rather proves my point,' he said tersely. 'Order the supper for us, will you? Anything will do. While we eat we'll get the roster sorted out.' Without a backward glance he left her to go to his own room.

A slow flush of humiliation spread hotly over her face and body. How typically male, the furious thought came to her, to kiss a woman because he wanted to, then somehow blame her, by being stand-offish, for both his desire and the fact that he had given in to it. In addition to that, he seemed to have deliberately misunderstood her last remark.

Absently she carried the empty mugs to the kitchen, feeling bewildered and frustrated. If she was honest with herself, and she was trying to be, she found him incredibly attractive. Yet she was mature enough that she could cope with it and still maintain a proper professional relationship.

Oh. . .to hell with him! There was no way that she was going to let the day end on this sour note, to let the discussion end there, which it would do if Owen were to sleep for several hours then do most of the night-shift. It could be a long time before there was a chance to clear the air after they had got the duty roster sorted out. Resolutely she first ordered the supper, then, steeling herself for an unpleasant encounter, marched to the door of his room and knocked.

'Come in.' The sound was muffled.

When she entered he was lying on the bed, facing away from her, then he turned towards her, propped up on one elbow. The room was dim, the shade drawn down, so it was clear to Alanna that he wanted to sleep and her nerve almost failed her.

'Owen. . .sorry to intrude. . .this won't take long. I . . . I don't want to have this. . .this animosity between us. I can't work like that, in an atmosphere that's less than cordial. We must sort this out. Now.' She moved closer to stand by the bed.

'How do you propose we should do that?' he asked, rolling over to face her.

'To. . .to just acknowledge that we are attracted to each other. . .that we aren't going to let it bother us. . . What does the odd kiss matter, now and again? It doesn't mean anything. You don't have to be so. . .sort of honourable and stuffy.' She paused, glad that he could not see her heated face in the dim room, feeling that perhaps she had not put that very well. . .

There was a stillness, when neither of them moved. Alanna felt her throat constrict. . .a fearful anticipation. Although she wanted to turn and leave the room, she felt rooted to the spot. Then, with a quick, fluid movement, Owen reached forward and grabbed her arm, pulling her down on to the bed beside him with seemingly effortless strength.

'Ah. . .' The cry escaped from her involuntarily as she lay stretched out full-length beside him, the breath knocked out of her, held by him with one arm. For a few moments he did nothing, waiting, watching. . . Very slowly he leaned over her and moved his mouth delicately across her lips several times, tantalisingly. . . then over her heated cheek to her ear, where with great finesse he used the tip of his tongue to explore its shell-like cavities and curves, barely touching her. Somewhere in the room a clock ticked. She felt shocked into a delicious immobility and silence.

At the soft, moist touch, a desire seemed to explode inside her with a force that left her feeling paralysed by its power. 'Don't. . .' The anguished whisper was forced from her, because she now realised her mistake; in an instant she knew that she had no resistance against him. How naïve she had been. . . She was no match for him. . .

The hand that she moved up frantically to push him away moved instead, as though of its own volition, to tangle with his hair. As his tongue persistently caressed her she became aware that her breath was coming in small moans that she seemed unable to control. When she felt that she could not tolerate the exquisite pleasure a moment longer, he brought his mouth down hard on hers in a sensual, demanding kiss. Passion mounted in her to match his, and she found herself returning his kisses with an equal, desperate fervour. It seemed that he was willing her, by the sheer power of his personality and his attraction, to give herself to him. All he had to do was take her.

When he drew away from her she lay with her head flung back weakly against his pillow, her hair spread out over it. 'Don't. . .' she murmured. 'Please. . .' Come back, come close, she wanted to say. Don't move away. . .

'You seem to have run out of adjectives, Miss Hargrove,' he said lightly, mockingly, his tone belied by his uneven breathing. 'Like "honourable" and "stuffy."' When he began to kiss her again, lightly, provocatively, she found herself pulling at his shirt, wanting to touch him. Obligingly he broke away briefly to take it off. When she made contact with his bare skin, tentatively touching his broad, smooth back with hands that were suddenly nervous, they both tensed with an unspoken anticipation.

'Do you still think this doesn't mean anything?' he said, his voice low.

What could she say, when she wanted so much to touch his warm skin?

'Hmm?' he persisted.

'Yes,' she lied, stubbornly refusing to give in.

'Really, Miss Hargrove?' The sarcasm was very deliberate.

'It doesn't have to. . .we can let it mean what we want it to mean.' Again she lied, feeling herself trembling, hoping that he was not aware of it. Intuitively she knew that her days of youthful insouciance were over, here, with this man. . .whatever the personal future might be for them. . .that she could be very, very hurt. Regardless, she took the initiative, pulling his head down to meet her lips, feeling him smile against her as he hungrily anticipated her.

One of the outside doors slammed, followed by a louder slam of the inner door.

'Grub up!' An unknown voice shattered the quiet of their retreat.

Owen began to laugh, his shoulders heaving as he lay above her. 'That'll be Joe, from the kitchen,' he explained, 'with our supper. He comes from the States originally. . .from Wyoming. Fancies himself as a sort of cowboy. . .minus the steers.' With ease he rolled off the bed and stood up. 'Don't go away, honey.'

Alanna lay in the warmth left by his body. She was coming to love his drawl, his low-key humour, even when it was at her expense.

At the door of the bedroom Owen shouted, 'Thanks, Joe!'

'No problem!' Joe called back. 'Don't let it get cold.' Two consecutive slams signalled his exit.

Owen came to sit on the edge of his bed. 'Well, Miss Hargrove, you seem to have taken over my bed. . .and I don't remember inviting you in.'

'Sorry. . .and don't call me Miss Hargrove!'

'Just trying to formalise the situation. . . So what did you really come here to tell me? That any sort of physical contact between us doesn't matter?' When she did not reply, he went on, 'And do you still think that? You don't seem to be quite so garrulous now.'

Still sitting on the edge of the bed, he turned towards

her and moved a hand under her shirt and sweater, moving cool fingers up towards her breasts where, with an experienced touch, he released the front closure of her bra to allow his hand to enclose her sensitive flesh, to move his thumb over her nipple, to produce in her the most exquisite sensations. . . With the other hand he touched her thigh, softly caressing her through the thin fabric of her jeans.

'Owen. . .please. . .' The cry broke from her after several seconds of such escalating pleasure that she knew she would soon lose all credibility with him.

'Please what?' he said, very slowly withdrawing his hands from her, kneading the soft skin of her narrow waist before he drew back from her, to sit regarding her in the dim light. 'Admit that you were wrong.'

Then she knew that in the last few moments he had deliberately teased her, had brought her to a fever pitch of longing so that he could leave her frustrated, just to make a point. . .to make it very clear to both of them.

Humiliation and frustration goaded her as she sat up, as she brought her arm back and swung it forward so that her hand made contact with his face in a sharp, stinging slap. All the built-up anger that had started with his verbal onslaught during their flight from Edmonton went into that gesture.

There was an awful silence in the room as he sat very still, and she strove to control her tumultuous breathing, fearful because she had acted out of character.

At last he spoke. 'How very banal, Alanna.' His voice was almost neutral, the anger well under control.

Near to tears, she got up and headed for the door, yanking it open almost to run to the sanctuary of her own small bedroom. Owen was close behind her, not letting her close the door, so that she was forced to retreat before him to the centre of the room.

'Alanna. . .'

'It's my turn now,' she confessed, wrapping her arms around her own body in a hug, 'to admit that I've behaved like an idiot. I'm sorry. . . To quote a Canadian expression, I seem to have been playing in the wrong league.'

'But I wanted you to kiss me. . . I needed that.' He was deliberately echoing the words that she had spoken earlier, rubbing salt in the wound, still teasing in a way that was becoming deadly serious.

'You don't have to be so. . .so arrogant. . .such an awful know-it-all. You wanted me, in spite of your sarcasm. . .'

'Sure I did. . .do. You're incredibly beautiful. . . delectable even. There's something about a beautiful woman who's also intelligent. . .especially if she's a little naïve. . .'

'Shut up!' If only she could tell him that she was Tim Cooke's sister, that she knew all about his ruthless techniques. The contained urge to do so was another source of tension for her.

'Come here,' he said softly.

'No, I. . . I don't think we ought to start again.'

'We're not going to. We'll come to an understanding. Just come here.' It seemed that he had got her just where he wanted her, that when the time was ripe, for him, after a suitable interval, they would become lovers. Apparently he took it for granted and, strangely, she did too. . . Stubbornly, perversely, she resolved to hold off as long as possible. . .

'Honey. . .' He held open his arms to her, his lean face serious, his eyes alight with a tense sexual desire for her that she had never before seen on the face of any man.

When she came to him he put his arms round her,

under her shirt, pulling her hard against him. 'I think you know that I want you. . .very, very much. But not yet. . .not after four days. . .' Now he was conciliatory, dissipating her resentment, yet contributing to her confusion.

'You must have thought me so blasé. . .' she said, gratified and chastened at the same time.

'No. . .delightfully innocent, maybe, but then you're entitled to be innocent.' As he spoke, he ended where he had begun, by moving his lips over the sensitive lobe of her ear, renewing the desire that had started this whole mess and which seemed to rob her of the ability to articulate.

'Owen. . .' she made an effort '. . .I want us to be friends. Is that naïve?'

'No. . . I think we're basically friends already. Agreed?'

'Yes. . .'

'Starting from tomorrow,' he said, 'I think we had better cool it for a few days.'

CHAPTER SIX

IT WAS clear by the beginning of the next week that he meant what he had said.

'Hey, have you two had a tiff or something, Alanna?' Bonnie Mae whispered as they sat together in the cramped office, taking a short coffee-break from the operating list on the Monday morning. 'Doc seems pretty formal all of a sudden.' She took a huge bite of a doughnut and chomped on it meditatively as she regarded Alanna with her usual candid stare.

'No, we haven't quarrelled. . .he's just keeping his distance. Apparently,' she whispered back, so that the object of their conversation should not hear, 'he wants to keep our relationship on a strictly professional footing, which is all right with me. It's a bit of an assumption on his part that it could be anything else.' Not an unfounded assumption, she admitted to herself, even as the half-truth left her lips.

'Isn't it just! That's men for you! Have a doughnut.' When Bonnie got up to pour herself another cup of coffee she looked outside the door, both ways, then came back. 'Listen, Alanna, don't you take any notice of him; he'll come round. It's that former fiancée of his, I guess; he had such an awful experience with her up here that he's wary of women doctors. His private life would have been OK, you can bet on that. . .at first!'

'Tell me about her. How did he get involved with her?' Alanna whispered back, curiosity overcoming her professional reticence. Not usually one to gossip, she felt instinctively that the nurse was not either. The aloofness that Owen Bentall had displayed to her that morning had been very apparent.

'Met her at medical school in Vancouver. Must have been some nepotism, if you ask me, for her to have got in there. Her name's Gloria Samantha.' Bonnie looked up to the ceiling in mock-horror. 'Bonnie Mae is bad enough. He must have had half a dozen others since her, looking the way he does. . .such a hunk! Comes up here to get away from them, I bet!' She giggled girlishly. 'Anyway, don't you worry. . . I know the doc pretty well. Behaving the way he does means he can't trust himself with you. . .not that he can't trust you!'

'Come on, Bonnie, back to the fray.' Alanna stood up, that last remark somehow lifting her spirits. 'Now, it's that debridement of leg next, I believe.' An operating list was posted on the wall of the office and she consulted it again. 'Yes, that's the old fish-hook injury. . . Mr Piot Lemieux. . .a Frenchman, by the sound of it.'

'Yep, that's it. Under general anaesthetic. A real mess, that one. Mr Lemieux's from Quebec, works on the boats. . .another great guy. Are you doing it, or is Doc?'

'We agreed that I would do it and he would give the anaesthetic. We're sort of alternating when we can.'

When the nurse had gone, walking swiftly with her characteristic rolling gait, like a sailor on a shifting deck, Alanna followed her with a muttered, 'I'll get scrubbed,' as Owen entered the office. She pushed past, brushing against him in her haste to get out of the room, her passing impression of him registering his raised eyebrows and watchful gaze.

'You don't mind doing the operation bit, Alanna?' he called after her as she moved in the direction of the operating-room.

'No. . .no.' There was nothing else to say, so she left him then to go to the scrub sinks. A week ago she might have thought his withdrawal somewhat amusing. Now it was no longer so. Confused about where they stood with each other, she thought it best just to get on with her job.

Over the weekend they had worked out a duty roster, which gave Owen Saturdays off and her Sundays, until further notice. They would each be on call alternate nights and every other weekend. On most Mondays, Wednesdays and Fridays they would have an all-day operating list, taking patients for day surgery. On the Tuesdays and Thursdays there would be outpatient clinics of various types. Home visits would be fitted in.

Any emergencies would take precedence over the routine work, of course. In addition to that, Owen would need to make some out-trips by plane to the area mines, to do routine health checks, to assess their first-aid equipment and procedures, and to do tetanus immunisations. One such trip was planned tentatively, for the following week. Alanna felt herself already looking foward to the breathing space.

The rest of the day passed uneventfully, their biggest case being the repair of a superficial hernia. Some of their patients had been flown in from the surrounding mines, for anything from a tooth extraction to the excision of an infected ingrowing toenail. Bit by bit Alanna was learning more about the community. Six months seemed such a short time, yet she doubted that she could tolerate being there long in the winter, when the days were dark, and exposed skin could freeze in a few seconds in the intense cold.

By the end of that second week the working relationship between the two doctors and the two nurses was easy and friendly, each individual having a pretty good idea of the strengths and weaknesses of the others professionally.

There had been time for her to explore the village on foot, when she had gone to the local grocery store. There was also a small art shop where local artisans sold their work. When the local people recognised her they were friendly and helpful, the children curious. They had seen many doctors come and go, mostly men, and accepted yet another new one with equanimity, resigned to the knowledge that she too would go.

'Do you want to come on rounds with me, Alanna?' Bonnie Mae had offered one day. 'It's time you went into a few homes. I've squared it with Doc. There's Mr Racine to see. . . Mr Q. . .then there's the fish-hook man, Piot Lemieux, to have a look at. . .not taking any chances with him, because he don't look after himself . . .then I want you to have a look at old Charlie Patychuk, with the pneumonia. He's on the mend. . . practically lives on antibiotics, but that chest of his is something else! Smokes like a chimney. What can you do about it, eh? He just shrugs when I tell him to quit, pretends he don't understand a word of English!'

'Patychuk? That's the boy's name. . .the one with the husky pup. Tommy Patychuk,' Alanna said.

'Yep. Old Charlie's his grandfather. They're very close, Tommy's always over at his grandpa's place, so maybe we can kill two birds with one stone. . .have a look at Tommy at the same time. They both need to come in for chest X-rays.'

The medical station skidoo subsided visibly and seemed to groan when Bonnie Mae swung herself on to it, so that Alanna, getting on behind her in the passenger seat, did so gingerly. Bonnie started the engine with her usual air of confidence, in the full expectation that it would carry them to their various destinations.

They arrived uneventfully at Charlie's place, their
first stop. He needed an injection of a long-acting
antibiotic to supplement what he was already taking by
mouth. Charlie was old and frail, confined to bed for
much of the day, living in a small wooden house with
his married daughter and her two children. Two fresh
caribou skins were pegged out on frames to dry in the
living-room. Alanna glanced at them curiously as she
and Bonnie passed through to the bedroom. People
here had few material possessions. Television kept
them in touch with an outside world that was largely
alien to their own. The old way of life, the hunting of
caribou, seal, walrus and polar bear, mingled with the
new life of electronic gadgetry and sophisticated
communications.

There was a fear among the native people that in a
few generations they would lose their skills of knowing
how to survive by living off the land. Coca Cola and the
skidoo threatened to take over. Some small communi-
ties were reverting to the dog sled and a number of
families in Chalmers Bay kept huskies. All this went
through Alanna's mind as she entered the bedroom
where the old man lay. He smiled at them from the bed,
displaying tobacco-stained teeth.

'Hello, Mr Patychuk,' Alanna greeted him, adding a
few of the sentences of Inuktitut that she had memorised, although he knew some English, having been a
guide to government officials in his younger days, so
Bonnie Mae had informed her earlier. He was a
diminutive man, shrunken and lined. Only his eyes,
shining like black coals, proclaimed a lively intelligence
and humour.

While Bonnie prepared the injection, Alanna took a
stethoscope from her medical bag to listen to his chest.
For years he had smoked and was now too old to take

any notice of admonitions from her to stop. Once this acute illness was over, no doubt, he would start puffing again.

'Take a quick breath, Mr Patychuk,' she instructed the old man as she placed the stethoscope on his chest, 'then give a cough.' As he coughed she could hear the rales in his chest, as well as the hollow breath sounds in between coughs, which were characteristic of tuberculosis. There seemed little doubt that he had pneumonia and pleurisy, with underlying chronic tuberculosis as well, which had been under control in the past but was probably flaring up again.

As Alanna moved the stethoscope slowly over different areas of his chest she considered that he might have lung cancer as well, brought on by years of smoking. She would arrange for him to be brought to the medical station for chest X-rays, which would then most likely have to be sent to a radiologist at the university hospital in Edmonton for interpretation.

From her medical bag she brought out a small sterile specimen bottle. 'I want you to cough up some sputum into this jar, Mr Patychuk.' She handed it to him. 'I want to send it down to Edmonton.' The mucus that he could cough up from his lungs would be able to tell them in the lab whether he had active tuberculosis, whether there were any cancer cells, possibly, or any bacterial infections still present.

Bonnie Mae listened to his chest as well, while Alanna made out the request forms to go with the specimen. 'He's much better than last time,' Bonnie assured Charlie's daughter who stood quietly watching them. 'He can get up for a while longer each day now, don't you agree, Alanna? It would be better if he didn't smoke again, of course.'

The daughter nodded in agreement, then shrugged

resignedly. Smoking was the only pleasure that he had, however dubious. He could no longer hunt.

As they were leaving, Tommy came in with his puppy in tow. He smiled shyly at Alanna and Bonnie, obviously pleased to see them. 'How's your pup, Tommy?' Alanna enquired, bending down to pet the young animal that gambolled around their legs.

'She's great. I'm teaching her to sit now. . .and I'm training her to take a harness. My father showed me how to do it. When she's older she can pull a sled,' he said, confident in his ability to train her, 'and she can be a lead dog. Females make the best lead dogs.'

'I hope you'll bring her to show us when she can pull a sled,' Alanna invited. 'I'd love to see it.'

'Sure,' he said proudly, 'if you're still in Chalmers Bay by then. I'll try to do it before the thaw.'

'We want to listen to your chest, Tommy,' Bonnie informed him, 'and we want you to come up to the clinic when your grandpa comes. You can both have a chest X-ray. We'll get Skip to pick you up in the truck later on this week. OK?'

'OK,' he said.

From there they went to visit a new-born baby and his mother, before going on to see Piot Lemieux, the fish-hook man.

On their second Friday in Chalmers Bay, Owen invited Alanna for a drink at the local bar, the Golden Nugget, in the evening, a deviation from his usual behaviour. By the time they were on their second drink they were chatting and sparring with each other verbally as though they had known each other much longer than just under two weeks.

'While I'm away at the Black Lake mine,' he reminded her, referring to his out-trip that started on

Monday, 'I can be contacted any time by radio telephone; those mining camps have first-class communications equipment. I can be on a plane back here within minutes of any call.'

'Yes. . . Bonnie Mae explained it all to me.'

'I don't want you to feel alone, as though I've deserted you after only two weeks. If I didn't think you were competent I wouldn't go so soon.'

'It's all right. . .really. I'm confident I can manage. I. . . I'll miss you, of course.' She watched his expression change after she had said that, his eyes darken. The atmosphere between them in the scruffy bar seemed suddenly electrified, so it was with mixed feelings of relief and thwarted longing on her part that their mutual regard was interrupted by a group of men who entered the room noisily and took over a nearby table, as though settling in for the evening, and they knew it was time for them to leave. Alanna had almost brought up the subject of his fiancée, former or otherwise; now there was no chance.

As they were walking back, the words of a childhood poem came to her, and she said them aloud:

'There are strange things done in the midnight sun,
By the men who moil for gold,
The Arctic trails have their secret tales,
That would make your blood run cold. . .'

'Well, well. . .you know Robert Service. I am surprised. . .the prim Miss Hargrove. . .' As they moved away from the feeble electric bulb that lighted the entrance to the Golden Nugget, Owen took her arm and tucked it beneath his own as they crunched and slithered to a wider path in the snow. There seemed to be no one else about, other than themselves, in the strange evening twilight.

'What do you mean prim?' she said indignantly, stumbling along, trying to match his more confident stride.

'You've called me "stuffy". . .as well as "arrogant", "pompous", and a "know-it-all". . .if I remember correctly. Just retaliating.'

'I'm not prim!' she insisted.

'Prove it to me some time,' he said.

That remark effectively silenced her for the moment. I thought I had, she wanted to say. By tacit agreement they walked out of their way to pass by the waterfront where an ice-breaker and another ship were moored in a channel of dark water. Further out they could discern large floating chunks of ice piled against each other, glowing eerily in the half-light. Beyond the channel lay the invisible islands—Victoria Island, Banks Island, Melville Island—and beyond them the permanent ice of the Arctic Ocean, on to the North Pole.

'The lights appear to be off,' Alanna said, preceding him into their sitting-room when they were back at the medical station, having flicked the light switch to no avail.

'Damn! There's a flashlight in the kitchen. . . I'll check the circuit-breakers. . .this happens quite frequently. Can you light a couple of candles? They're in the drawer under the coffee-table, with the matches.'

After much fumbling, she got the candles alight, then took off her outdoor clothing.

'The breakers are OK.' Owen returned to join her, peeling off his outer clothing as he did so. 'It must be a central problem. If it gets really cold in here we can always cuddle up together.' In the warm yellow circle of candlelight he dominated the room, making her more than ever aware of him. Already the room was cooler than usual. Above the dancing candle-flames their eyes met.

'I. . .was thinking that I should call Bonnie to see if the power is off over there. . .'

'It isn't.' He came to stand near her, looking down at her, his eyes roving over her tumbled hair that shone a burnished copper in the yellow light. 'I noticed when we came in.'

A *frisson* went through her even before he touched her and she steeled herself to withstand his attraction. The alcohol that he had consumed had obviously lowered his inhibition where she was concerned. Then when he touched her ice-cold cheek with a warm hand, brushing back her hair away from her face, her heart began to pound with the familiar, half-fearful anticipation.

'If I were to tell you what I'm thinking,' he said softly, 'you could sue me for sexual harassment in the workplace.'

'In that case,' she quipped, 'if we can be condemned by our thoughts, you should know that I could have been charged with murder where you are concerned. . . several times.'

The wry half-smile on his lips broadened as his hand moved to the back of her neck, pulling her towards him. 'I'll take a chance. . .seeing that you're unarmed. . . Kiss me, Alanna; I've wanted you for the last two hours. . .' He was tense, waiting for her to make the next move.

Remembering the feel of his lips when he had kissed her before, how they had lain together on his bed, she felt herself swaying forward against him, raising her face to his. When her lips were close to his, he put his mouth on hers, and her arms encircled his neck. The kiss was demanding, his firm mouth teasing her soft lips so that she felt she was drowning in a strange, enveloping warmth, where she could not move. . .

'I want to make love to you. . .' The words were slurred as he spoke them against her cheek, so that she was not sure she had heard them. 'Come to bed with me. . . Alanna?' There was no mistaking the expression on his face, even if she chose to pretend that she had not heard the words. . .did not know how to deal with her own flare of desire.

'His private life would have been OK, you can bet on that.· . .' The remembered words of Bonnie Mae came then to haunt her. Owen would have stood in this room with his fiancée, perhaps uttering the same words. . . would most certainly have taken Gloria — willingly, it seemed — to bed. Perhaps Gloria had taken the initiative. Did she want to follow the pattern? The frantic question sounded in her brain, vying with the dictates of her body. It would be so easy to say yes, because that was what she wanted.

Deliberately she pulled his head down to her. Moving her lips on his as provocatively as she knew how, she kissed him long and deeply until she felt him shaking with desire for her, a deep internal trembling to match her own. She wanted to have something to remember of him if their relationship turned sour. . .when he found out that she was Tim Cooke's sister. . .

Summoning all her self-control and common sense, she extricated herself from his arms, putting some distance between them: 'This is not the right time, not when we've both been drinking. I'm sorry, Owen. . .'

His eyes narrowed with amazement as he confronted her, his chest rising and falling rapidly. 'If this isn't the right time, when will there be a right time?'

'I. . .don't know.'

'I didn't want this.' His tone was urgent now. 'But

now it's happened, we might as well accept it. From the time I saw you on that flight. . .knew who you were. . . it was inevitable.'

'You didn't know all of it. . .' She would have to tell him about Tim.

The kitchen telephone rang, startling them back to the reality of the unheated room. Sluggishly she moved to answer it.

'Is the power off over there, you guys?' Bonnie Mae's voice queried.

'Yes, it is, Bonnie.'

'Just had a call to say that a cable was down. It should be fixed within the next fifteen minutes or so. The two of you can come over to my place if it's kinda cool over there. You do have a kerosene heater in a cupboard. . . Doc knows where it is, although I don't suppose he'll let on about it if he wants to keep you warm himself!' Bonnie Mae's throaty chuckle would normally have found a response in her.

'That's a little too close to the mark, Bonnie,' she said feelingly, thinking of Gloria Samantha. 'Thanks for telling us. Bye.'

Owen stood in the doorway, his hands gripping the frame on either side. 'Well?'

Before she could anticipate him he had pulled her into his arms, his hands had found the bare skin beneath her enveloping sweater and he was kissing her hungrily in a way that destroyed all resistance. In moments she was clinging to him, all else forgotten. As he began to undress her in the cold room, she helped him, wanting his hands on her. . .then tremblingly pushed his shirt over his broad, muscular shoulders.

'You want me. . .admit it!' Insistently he forced a response from her.

'Yes. . .'

When the loud banging came on the outer door she stood almost naked in his entwining arms, shielded by his warmth from the encroaching cold.

'Who the hell. . .?' He groaned, moving away from her reluctantly. When he went to answer the door she quickly gathered up her clothes and practically ran to her room. Men's voices penetrated her sanctuary as, with shaking hands, she clicked the lock in place. Considerably later, when she heard the light, persistent knocking on her door, she stayed resolutely in the shower with the bathroom door open so that he could not fail to hear the running water, using the hot, cascading stream as a poor substitute for the warm arms of the man she wanted more than anything else in the world.

CHAPTER SEVEN

OWEN was out a lot over the weekend, sleeping late on the Saturday when she was on duty, then going out later in the day. Then on the Sunday it was her turn to be off, to go to the little Anglican church, while he spent most of his time over at the clinic. When they did meet face to face she greeted him with a certain stiffness that she could not shake off, and he answered with a controlled politeness.

It was just as well perhaps that neither of them had any vibes concerning the next few days, for Alanna might have been worrying for the entire weekend, waiting for all hell to break loose. As it was, the internal telephone buzzed at one o'clock in the morning, Monday, waking her from a peaceful sleep. Instantly alert, she swung herself out of bed, preferring to take any call in a standing position, ready to go.

'Dr Hargrove,' Bonnie Mae's worried voice came loud in her ear, 'there's a kid on his way over here with his parents. . .five years old. . .having trouble breathing. It sounds bad. I spoke to the mother on the phone. Apparently he's had a sore throat since yesterday and a bit of a fever, then in the evening his temperature shot up. They thought they could cope with it on their own, but just in the last half-hour he's been having trouble breathing and his colour's not good. I told them to get over here right away.'

As Bonnie spoke, Alanna thought quickly, her mind running ahead to what she would have to do. Momentarily she thought of calling Owen to help, then decided

107

that she would look at the boy first and assess the situation. He could be over to the clinic in a few minutes if necessary.

'Bonnie, we'll see the boy in the operating-room, just in case. I want the paediatric tracheostomy set, a laryngoscope, a set of small endotracheal tubes and the flexible bronchoscope. Have the emergency tracheal trocar ready; if it's acute epiglottitis I'll have to go in straight away to establish an airway before he suffocates. That's the first priority. Then we'll need an IV . . .normal saline. . .and an IV antibiotic. If you have time before I get there, draw me up some Xylocaine, one per cent plain, in a syringe.'

'Will do, Dr Hargrove. I'm on my way.'

Alanna let herself quietly out of the door into the covered walkway. Then she began to run, her footsteps pounding hollowly on the wooden floor of the narrow passage. She knew that the onset of acute epiglottitis was very sudden, that a child could be dead very quickly as the epiglottis swelled in response to an acute infection, blocking the throat so that no air could enter the lungs.

Get the airway open, put in the trocar above the sternum. . .take care not to go right through the trachea. . .very easy to do in a child. . .ease up on the pressure. . .take care to avoid the thyroid gland. . . don't want an acute thyroid crisis. What is the treatment for that? The commands in her mind came thick and fast. Have the suction ready, get the mucus out, get the oxygen connected. . .

Bonnie Mae was there ahead of her. The fact registered as she rushed into the operating-room. 'I'm opening up the tracheostomy set,' the nurse said tersely. 'The trocar's here too, and the flexible bronchoscope.' As she spoke she moved with speed, methodically opening the sterile tray on top of a small wheeled trolley, then she filled a syringe with local anaesthetic. 'I haven't checked the anaesthetic machine yet, Doc. It was all in order last night.'

'I'll do that, Bonnie. I'll need a throat swab too, for the lab, please.' As she moved over to check the sterile tracheostomy set-up, they heard the sound of a skidoo pulling up to the medical station outside. That would be the parents with the child.

'I'll bring in the kid, Doc, if you could just make sure there's everything here you're going to need.'

'All right, Bonnie. I'll be ready.'

One look at the child's face as Bonnie carried him quickly into the operating-room, followed by the distraught parents, told Alanna that the situation was indeed critical. His face was a deep grey-blue from lack of oxygen, his mouth wide open and his tongue protruding as he gasped ineffectually for air. Too frightened to cry, preoccupied with the effort to breathe, the little boy stared at Alanna with wide, terrified eyes.

Normally no one from outside would be allowed in the operating-room, but now neither Bonnie nor Alanna was going to stand on ceremony as the parents entered. It was doubtful that they could have kept them out. They were not native, most likely from down south. As Bonnie placed the little boy directly on the operating table, they moved to stand by him protectively, clutching at his small, inert hands. They obviously feared for his life.

'Now you lie there, John,' Bonnie soothed the boy. 'Everything's going to be just fine. Mum and Dad are going to stay right here with you.'

'Hello, I'm Dr Hargrove.' Alanna addressed the parents and then looked at the boy. It would have been better if she had called Owen in the beginning, she could see that now, but it was too late; there was not even time to go to the phone. Then she remembered that there was an emergency button that would ring a bell in the annexe, so that whoever was there would come instantly, no questions asked. 'Press the buzzer please, Bonnie,' she added quietly to the nurse.

She put on a pair of sterile gloves from the trolley. 'John, I'm going to put a little tube into your neck so that you can breathe. It won't take long and I'm going to put some medicine in your skin first so that you won't feel anything. All you have to do is lie still.'

Bonnie, having jammed in the emergency button, came to stand near Alanna. 'Now, Mother,' she said firmly to the boy's mother, 'you stand up here near the top of the table and hold John's head. . .put a hand either side of his head, like this; just hold him gently but firmly so that he doesn't move while the Doc here gets in the local, then the tube. OK? Now, Dad,' she addressed the father, 'you just hold his hands. . .like so . . .that's great! Now I'll just take care of the suction and the oxygen, then we're all set to go. Ready, Dr Hargrove?'

The boy's painfully laboured breathing was the only sound in the room as Alanna picked up the syringe with the local anaesthetic. It was good psychology on Bonnie Mae's part to involve the parents, as well as the fact that their practical help was needed. The mother stood rigidly, holding the boy's head, her lips compressed, fighting back tears. The silent father held the boy's hands.

'Just a little prick first, like a mosquito bite,' she said, bending over him, holding the syringe so that he could not see it. 'Everything's going to be all right, John. Pass me one of those alcohol swabs, please, Bonnie; I haven't got time to prep the skin.' As she felt for the top end of the sternum where she was to inject, she had a mental impression of Owen dressing hurriedly in the annexe. She wished he were there beside her. The boy only flinched slightly as she injected the local, with no energy to cry.

With the trocar and cannula—which was specially designed for this purpose—held in her right hand, she palpated the small trachea with the fingers of her left hand. The sharp trocar had to be forced through the skin and tissue of the neck, into the trachea, to effect an immediate airway for the boy who was very rapidly suffocating. 'Stand by with the suction, Bonnie,' she said quietly, without looking up, 'then the oxygen.'

'Gottcha, Doc. Hold firmly, Mother.'

Alanna pushed the trocar, with its surrounding cannula, into the boy's fragile neck, then withdrew it, leaving the cannula in place. A sigh escaped both her and the nurse as there was a rush of air through the open cannula when the patient's small chest strained again to breathe. Bonnie quickly and expertly inserted a plastic suction tube into the opening while Alanna continued to hold it in place. There was a satisfying sucking noise as mucus that had partially blocked the airway was sucked out.

'Oxygen now, Bonnie. . .quickly.' Alanna's voice was high with tension. The worst part was over, but they were not out of the woods. Alanna gave the child several blasts of oxygen through a tubing connected to the cannula. Almost instantly the little boy's skin tone changed from greyish blue to pink, bringing a gasp of relief from his mother.

'Thank God. Oh, thank God,' the mother whispered. Then the tears came, cascading unheeded down her face, and her hands moved to stroke her son's small arms. John lay quietly, as though he knew what he had to do to co-operate, knew that the immediate crisis was over, his expressive eyes fixed on his mother's face.

Alanna looked up then. Owen had come unnoticed into the room and was standing quietly watching the scene. At the sight of him, she felt some of the tension drain from her. 'Owen——' she turned to him, still holding on to the cannula '—would you put in an IV, please? Sorry to get you up. I'm going to need a bit of help.'

'That's OK. I was awake anyway. I heard you running along the passage, so I knew something was up.' He came to the operating table, gave an acknowledging smile to the parents, before turning his attention to the boy. 'It looks as though you did a very good job, Alanna. I'll help you get the tracheostomy tube in. . . the IV first, I think.'

'Yes. . .thank you. I would like to take a throat swab too; there wasn't really time to do that first.'

She watched him while he took an angiocath and inserted it into a vein in the back of the boy's hand, with Bonnie's help. In the bad old days, not so long ago, this child and others like him would very probably have died *en route* to the city, or before he even got on a plane, unless a nurse could have managed to put in a tube. In a few minutes she and Owen would insert a more permanent tubing through which the boy would breathe for the next week or so, until his fever was down and the infection completely gone. They would send a throat swab to the lab in the city to determine exactly what organism was responsible for the infection.

When they had done all that they could do in the operating-room, the boy was transferred to the recovery-room, together with the parents, who had elected to remain with him at least until the morning.

When he was settled, immediately drifting off into an exhausted sleep, Owen took Alanna's arm.

'Come. . .' He drew her gently out of the room. 'I'm going to make us all a cup of coffee in the office. Come with me.' Obediently she followed him, leaving their patient in the care of Bonnie Mae. The tiny office was warm and cosy, with its potted plants and coloured postcards on the cork noticeboard juxtaposed with the work paraphernalia. Owen looked dishevelled, the collar of his white coat tucked under from having been hastily put on, a stubble of dark hair on his face.

'Might as well give the parents a cup of coffee too. You sit down, Alanna, I want to discuss my trip. I don't think I ought to go to the mine today; it can be put off for a few more days until the boy's on the mend. He'll obviously need round-the-clock supervision, and we can't expect Bonnie to do more than her fair share. We could ship him off to the city, but I'm sure he would much rather be here with his parents. We'll get that swab out on the morning plane.'

'I would prefer that myself, too,' she said. There seemed to be something else on his mind. Alanna watched him closely as he made the coffee. She was thoughtful when he left the room temporarily to take three mugs of coffee out to Bonnie Mae and the parents. What now?

When he came back he immediately enlightened her. 'I want to apologise for being so boorish on the flight from Edmonton to here. I made a lot of assumptions that I shouldn't have made. You're clearly a very good doctor, and I had no right to put you down. . .if mainly by implication. I guess I did jump to conclusions. It's a little late for an apology, I know. . .'

'I do understand.' An impishness impelled her to add, 'You had a bad experience, so I was told. Something to do with a fiancée. . .by the name of Gloria Samantha?'

A look of shock momentarily passed across his features while she sanguinely sipped her coffee, daring to meet those astute grey eyes that seemed able to read her mind. Then, to her relief, he laughed with genuine amusement and self-mockery.

'Bonnie Mae's been gossiping evidently,' he said ruefully, 'and indulging in a little amateur psychology as well. Yes, I did have a fiancée once. . .sort of. We decided to get engaged before coming up here. . . mainly her idea. It seemed more convenient that way at the time. It was a mistake. Does that satisfy your curiosity?'

Alanna slowly added another spoonful of sugar to her coffee to delay her answer. 'We weren't gossiping. . .' A flush crept over her cheeks as he watched her. 'It was just something that came up naturally in a conversation. Bonnie noticed that you were being rather — er — hostile to me; hence the amateur psychology.'

'Well, there may be some truth in her assessment, plus the fact that Gloria was a bloody awful doctor. I'm not judging her because she's a woman. . . I've met some pretty awful doctors of both sexes. Anyway, she's subsequently taken on dermatology as a specialty. One can't go far wrong with acne.' He took a swallow of coffee. 'And just so that you get the complete picture, yes, we did sleep together. She's a beautiful woman and it helped to fill the long nights up here. Once she got back to Vancouver she promptly married someone else.'

Alanna's face flamed. 'I didn't mean to pry. I'm sorry.'

'It's OK. I always like to know what's being said

about me behind my back. I prefer that it be the truth. Apart from the bed thing, she wasn't of much use. I can see that you are going to be quite the opposite. . .for which I should be truly thankful, I guess.' He stood up. 'Anway, I hope you'll accept my apology, Alanna. Let's get back to our patient, shall we?'

The thought that she had invaded Owen's privacy by being flippant stayed with Alanna for a long time, so that she was glad she had to be up all night with the boy while her two colleagues slept. At breakfast-time, after Bonnie Mae had reappeared, she managed to avoid him. After only four hours' sleep, she felt like a zombie as they commenced the operating list on Monday morning.

In anticipation that Owen would be away at the Black Lake mine, they had booked a short operating list of very minor cases, which was just as well now that Bonnie Mae had to spend most of her time with the little boy and his tracheostomy. Mr Racine had been discharged home. Today they had called in a nursing aide again from the village to help with the bedside nursing so that Bonnie Mae could do other things when necessary. Skip hurried around in high gear, doing everything himself, getting each case ready, trying to be all things to all people, until Owen told him that they could manage without a scrub nurse. The day wore on and gradually they got through the cases, helping each other.

Having been conscious over the past week that Owen had been avoiding her at times, while obviously drawn to her at other times, there was a supreme irony in the present reality that she now wanted to avoid him until she could overcome a sense of embarrassment. His proximity, as they bent over each patient at the operating table, heightened her awareness of him to a fever pitch, so that she found herself fumbling the instruments and being less than steady when putting in sutures.

He was more than usually silent too. Occasionally she would look up and find him staring at her, unsmiling, the set of his mouth hidden by the mask that he wore. Neither of them could think of much to say. Alanna felt sure that he must know of the uncomfortable warmth that invaded her being every time they inadvertently touched, and she chided herself for being so gauche.

At lunchtime she ate quickly in the office, then went to see John. The little boy was doing well, a good colour, the fever down, obviously responding to the antibiotic. They kept him under mild sedation so that he would not be too anxious about having to breathe through a tube in his neck. She read the nurse's notes and made some of her own. When they were preparing for the last patient, standing side by side at the scrub sink, Owen eventually spoke to her.

'You might as well get some sleep after this.'

'Yes. . .'

'I'll take the night-shift, if you could relieve Bonnie for a few hours this evening after you've slept.'

'All right. . .thank you,' she mumbled, keeping her eyes on her arms as she soaped them at the sink.

'Let's hope we don't get any more cases in the night.'

'Yes. . .'

It was Thursday before Owen finally took a plane out of Chalmers Bay to go to the Black Lake lead-zinc mine, planning to be back some time during the day on Saturday. Before he left they discussed the boy and how to manage him, agreeing that they would leave the tracheostomy tube in place a few days longer. 'Call me, Alanna, if you're worried about anything. . . OK?' He smiled at her warmly, as though there really had been no awkwardness between them, before he departed. With mixed feelings Alanna watched the skidoo, with Skip at the controls, take her partner swiftly away from the medical station in the direction of the airstrip.

Later in the morning she saw Lynne Nanchook, the pregnant woman, again. Lynne brought her young son, a toddler, with her this time, who was a little too big to be carried in his mother's *amauti*, the roomy parka that had a back-pouch for carrying a baby and a hood to pull over the heads of mother and child. Instead, he was bundled up in a little snowsuit of his own. As Alanna looked at him he turned his head shyly into his mother's chest so that his face was hidden, then clung to her hand as Alanna examined her.

'Do you know yet if I will have to go to the city?' Lynne enquired anxiously as Alanna once again palpated her swollen abdomen and then moved the foetal stethoscope into position to hear the baby's heartbeat. 'You see my son. . .how he not want to let me out of his sight. . . He would be so upset if I go.'

'Yes, well. . .at the moment the baby is lying with its bottom downwards, what we call a breach presentation, which is all right at this stage of the pregnancy, but later on it is better if the baby turns so that the head is coming first. Sometimes the baby doesn't turn because the head is too big to fit down into the pelvis. . .which could mean that your bones in the pelvis are too narrow to let the baby come out easily. That's what we call disproportion; it's something that we have to watch out for in your case, because that is what happened last time with your son.'

'Yes. . . I was hoping this time would be different.'

'Well, it's still early days. Try not to worry too much about it now.' Alanna smiled at her and the little boy, who now had his hooded head buried against his mother's encircling arm. 'Plan to go to the city, have your bag packed in plenty of time, but it's by no means decided yet.'

Lynne sighed. 'OK,' she said resignedly, getting up clumsily from the couch.

'Come to the clinic again in two weeks' time. Perhaps the baby will have turned by then. After that, I would like to see you once a week. Everything is fine. . .your blood-pressure, the baby's heart-rate. So try not to worry.' As Lynne departed, Alanna herself felt worried. Beneath the young woman's reluctant acceptance of the situation, Alanna sensed a desperate resistance to leaving Chalmers Bay when the time came, which had to be at least a week before she was due to go into labour. It was understandable.

That afternoon there was a paediatric clinic, during which she and Bonnie Mae were particularly alert for signs of throat infections in any of the babies and young children.

'This place is feast or famine, Alanna,' the nurse said to her in the evening, prior to the late shift to take care of John, their one in-patient. 'Maybe after this we'll have a long run with nothing much doing. Let's hope, eh? Then we can all catch up on some sleep.'

'Yes,' Alanna agreed. 'I'll relieve you later, Bonnie.'

The living quarters were peculiarly silent and bereft when Alanna let herself into the sitting-room, so that she quickly turned on the radio. Even when Owen had been avoiding her it had been nice to know that he was around. As she prepared her own supper, a statistic that she had been given during her orientation period came to mind — in the vast province where she was working there was only one doctor for every eleven hundred of population, and of those doctors less than ten were specialists, in a total population of a little more than fifty-two thousand.

Now that Owen was temporarily away, she had a vision of all eleven hundred patients, for whom she was statistically responsible, descending on Chalmers Bay medical station at the same time, coming by plane, ship and dog sled. Although there were only about three thousand people permanently in Chalmers Bay itself, all the mining and oil exploration added largely to the population of the area and the possibility of accidents. Alanna felt somewhat vulnerable as she ate her supper alone, knowing herself to be the last line of defence.

The early morning presented the perfect opportunity to take a look at the file of Tim's patient. There was no lock on the tall cupboard that held the files. A small card index sat on the centre shelf, while all the manila folders were numbered. Alanna ran her fingers quickly over the file index, which was arranged in alphabetical order, with the uncomfortable feeling that she was doing something clandestine. Don't be ridiculous, she told herself; you have every right to go through the files. . . At the same time she would have felt better if she had told Owen and Bonnie Mae about her relationship to Tim Cooke.

She found that the file was empty, apart from two photocopied sheets of basic information. There was nothing at all about the Caesarian section that the woman had undergone at the medical station. Alanna stared at them in disappointment.

The first two babies had been delivered by Caesarian section at a hospital in Edmonton several years before, the mother having been flown there the first time because of antenatal complications. It had been planned that the third baby, the one that Tim had been concerned with, should be dealt with in the same way. Although Tim had explained all that, she had wanted to see the notes first-hand and perhaps make copies. That mother had been more or less in the same situation as Lynne Nanchook.

'What's up, Alanna?' Bonnie Mae's booming voice made her jump guiltily. 'What you doing here so early?'

'Oh, hello, Bonnie.' Alanna looked up at the nurse who was coming towards her. 'Just checking up on something. How's John this morning?'

'He's fine. That tracheostomy tube will just about be ready to come out when Doc's back on Saturday. It could actually come out now, in my opinion. Want some coffee? I'm just about to make some. Nuna from the village came in early to relieve me. I'm parched.'

'Thanks. I'd like some coffee.'

'What are you looking at?' With characteristic curiosity, Bonnie Mae squeezed in beside Alanna to look over her shoulder, then reached out to turn over the sheets of paper. 'Gee! That's the inquiry case, isn't it? The one with Tim Cooke and Clinton Debray — that awful guy!'

'Yes, it is, Bonnie.' Alanna flushed as Bonnie Mae looked from the chart to her, then she made a quick decision. 'I might as well tell you. . . Tim Cooke is my brother. My half-brother. I should have told you earlier, I suppose, only I thought it might be a bit awkward for everyone. It was just that I didn't want Owen Bentall to know. . .not yet. You see, I want to make a few enquiries of my own. Tim feels that he was treated unfairly in this case, that he did all he could and that Dr Debray overruled him, then tried to arrange things so that Tim took most of the blame after the baby was born dead.'

'Geez! Fancy that! You being the sister, I mean. You always have reminded me of him; I put it down to the accent. Yeah, it was a funny case. The nurse who was up here at the time told me all about it; she supported Tim, you know. I was on vacation, then sick leave. That Clinton Debray. . .he's a weird one! He'd swear that black was white to cover himself. What are you trying to find out exactly? It looks as though all the pertinent info is missing. . .must be at the district coroner's office.'

'Tim told me that he had radioed out from here to try to contact any passing aircraft, or any radio station that could contact one for him. He can't prove that, although he said he did make a momentary contact with someone — he doesn't know who. You see, he wanted to get the woman flown out immediately. Dr Debray was against it. . .to save money, or something; he said she was in false labour.'

'Yeah, sounds like him. What a lulu!'

'Anyway, Tim can't prove that he wanted to get her out early. The controller at the airstrip denied that he'd been asked to keep trying to contact any aircraft in the vicinity.'

'Yeah. . .' Bonnie Mae was thoughtful.

'You see, Tim was really upset about the way it all turned out.' Alanna did not elaborate on the way the locals concerned had all closed ranks to shift the blame to him, the outsider, determined as they were to accord blame. Although Owen Bentall had tried to be impartial when he had been called in, so Tim had said, he had not been sympathetic. 'He feels that if he could somehow prove that he made radio contact he might be able to prove his case, recoup some of his self-esteem. He's

been more or less officially exonerated, but still. . .'
Her voice trailed off. There was no way that she could
really explain how the inquiry had affected Tim's
personal and professional confidence. And he had
become obsessed with a need to prove and record the
truth.

'Come into the office,' Bonnie Mae offered. 'We can
talk while I make the coffee.'

'Tim didn't get a chance to make copies of his notes,'
Alanna began again once they were settled in the office,
now feeling a strong need to talk about everything that
she had kept bottled up for so long, 'they were
impounded. . .by Owen Bentall, as a matter of fact. . .
so I was hoping that they had been returned.'

'Seems to me,' said Bonnie Mae, busying herself with
the coffee things, 'that no one made any attempt to find
out if Dr Cooke tried to make radio contact with
anyone. They had to do the operation anyway, eventually, because of foetal distress.'

'Yes. . .' There was a tight feeling in Alanna's throat.
The full realisation of what Tim had come through was
very immediate. It had happened right here. 'Apparently, the woman herself didn't want any sort of fuss
afterwards; she hadn't wanted a third baby so soon after
the second one. So sad. . .'

'So I heard. Here, have some coffee.'

'Thanks.' Alanna took the proffered mug, forced
herself to sip the hot liquid.

'Is that why you came here, Alanna. . .because of all
this with Dr Cooke?' Bonnie heaved her bulk up on to
the desk, to sit with legs dangling.

'Partly; certainly I might not have come
otherwise. . .'

'I thought not.' Bonnie Mae looked at her shrewdly.
'You're too good a calibre of doctor to bury yourself up

here. You could take your pick of jobs anywhere, I bet. Apart from Dr Bentall and people like Tim Cooke, we don't attract the best people up here. Too bad really, because we desperately need good people. Maybe things will change now with this new scheme by the NMDC.'

'You're trying to flatter me, Bonnie,' Alanna smiled, embarrassed. 'What happened to De Debray after he left here?'

'I'm not flattering you. He's disappeared into the woodwork, from what I hear. He won't be hired up here again.'

'What about you, Bonnie?' Alanna wanted to shift the focus away from herself. 'You're a super nurse; what keeps you in the North?'

'Ah, well. . .' Bonnie Mae's eyes glazed over as though she were contemplating far horizons. 'Two main reasons, I guess. One. . .it's a challenge, and I like a challenge. I can use everything I ever learned up here and learn more all the time. Two. . .it's also because of Chuck, my boyfriend. He's in this area, he's a pilot with a charter company, based in Inuvik and Edmonton. He's in Chalmers more than anywhere else, doing a lot of runs for the mining companies. We plan to marry as soon as we've saved enough money for him to start his own small charter business when the time's right.'

'I see. I admire your stamina. You're very brave.'

'I'm not really. I get plenty of time off. It's the thought of Chuck that keeps me going. He stays with me in my quarters. It's a great arrangement. If I were in the city I'd see him much less.' She fingered the diamond ring that she always wore on the gold chain around her neck.

'Bonnie, please don't tell Owen Bentall that I'm Tim

Cooke's sister. . .not yet. I will tell him, of course, when I'm ready.'

'OK, Alanna. He can be rather judgemental, I know. Look. . . I was thinking. . .perhaps Chuck can check up on that radio call your brother made, if you know the date and the approximate time. Chuck knows most of the guys at the weather stations around here. Some of them have their own equipment that they use in their spare time; they're radio hams, always trying to make contacts around the world. Maybe one of them picked up something.'

'That would be great if he could do that, Bonnie. Thank you.'

'He'll be calling me this morning early. I'll get on to it right away.'

It had been a satisfying day, Alanna conceded later as she ate an early supper by herself in the sitting-room of the annexe. She had opened a half-bottle of a light, dry white wine that had been nicely cooling in the snow outside the door, one of the bottles that Owen had brought with him. Through the window she could see to Coronation Gulf, where a pile of huge, irregular chunks of ice had been pushed up on to the shore by the ice-breaking ship. Soon it would be melting slowly. Already it seemed to have got smaller since she last stared out of the window.

She and Bonnie Mae had delivered a baby in the late afternoon, her first in Chalmers Bay. The mother and baby would stay at the clinic for forty-eight hours, taken care of by Nuna the nursing aide, then they would go home, where they would be visited by a doctor or a nurse once a day for the next two weeks. All was quiet now at the clinic. Bonnie Mae had gone off duty. Skip had been asked to do a rare night-shift with their little tracheostomy patient, whose mother was with him too. When the internal phone rang she went to answer it with a certain apprehension.

'You want to come out to the bar, Alanna, with me and Chuck? He just turned up. There's a visiting entertainer tonight at the Golden Nugget; it's Yodelling Joe. . .he's pretty good.'

'Yodelling Joe?' Alanna laughed with relief. 'That's not the Joe who works in the kitchen, by any chance?'

'No, though I bet he could yodel if he tried! He seems able to do everything else! Out East they have Stompin' Tom Connors, out here we have Yodelling Joe. How about it? We'll take the beeper, and Skip can call us on that if he has to.'

'I'd love to go, Bonnie. Thanks.'

'Pick you up in about fifteen minutes. Chuck has his own skidoo.'

'So this is what you get up to while I'm away!'

Alanna came to a halt just inside the door of the annexe, her carefree mood suspended, as she returned from the bar at about half-past nine to be met by Owen Bentall, a sardonic smile on his face that was not entirely welcoming. Neither was the censure in his tone altogether joking.

'Owen. . .what are you doing here?' Alanna was puzzled. Her heart had given an instant lurch of recognition at the sound of his voice. 'You're not due back until late tomorrow. Why did you come back early?' A familiar tension eased aside the gaiety that the evening's entertainment had engendered.

'It was a last-minute thing. There was an unexpected flight out, so I took it. Everything I had to do was finished.' Owen stood in the sitting-room, dressed casually, looking tired. A dark stubble covered the lower half of his face. The remains of a meal on the table had joined the plate, glass and wine bottle that she had left behind. The wine bottle was now empty.

Alanna slipped out of her parka and boots. 'Bonnie and Chuck took me to hear Yodelling Joe,' she explained, smiling at the memory of it. 'Certainly an experience I wouldn't have wanted to miss. Some of the RCMP officers were there. . .a few familiar faces.'

It was good to see Owen. To cover a sudden urge to fling her arms around his neck, she busied herself transferring the used crockery from the table to the kitchen. 'How was everything at the mine?'

'Fine. . . You shouldn't get too involved with any of the guys around here, you know. . .' He left the words hanging in the air, as he stood with hands in trouser pockets, looking at her broodingly. 'With them, what you see is what you get, mostly. . .'

'Yes, I know,' she said. 'I've no intention of getting "involved". It's not your business anyway, is it?' In fact, the bar had been so noisy that she had scarcely exchanged two sentences with anyone other than Bonnie and Chuck.

'I've seen some very unfortunate and inappropriate liaisons between men and women up here, because of the loneliness. Liaisons that would never hold up once they returned to their usual lives.'

'Yes, quite! I can imagine,' she replied curtly.

'To a certain extent, I feel responsible for you,' he said, fixing her with an intent stare.

'Oh, yeah!' She borrowed one of his phrases, unable to keep the irony out of her voice. 'Don't worry, I'm ever mindful that I'm here temporarily.'

'Good.'

'Why did you come back early? Didn't you trust me

to hold the fort?' Alanna could not keep a certain bitterness out of her voice.

Owen followed her to the kitchen, lounging in the doorway. 'As I said, there was an unexpected flight, that's all. Not quite all, perhaps. . . I did miss you.'

'Oh. . .well.' She fiddled around with the crockery in the sink, running hot water over it. 'So did I miss you. It's. . .it's strange being in a place with no roads out; one feels sort of claustrophobic. . .trapped. When you're here I don't think about it too much.'

'Yes, I know.' He stood looking at her consideringly. 'Actually, more pertinent. . .while you were out, your patient over there had a slight post-partum haemorrhage.'

'Oh, no!' Alanna dropped the cutlery she was holding with a clatter, a sense of something like horror replacing the feeling of warmth that his admission of having missed her had roused. The chart that she had read that morning of her brother's patient had sensitised her to possible disasters, to the spectre of inquiries. Perhaps Owen was taking a sadistic pleasure in suddenly bringing her down to earth.

'Why didn't you tell me earlier? Were they trying to get me at the bar? I did have the beeper with me.' A sense of guilt at having gone out engulfed her. 'I shouldn't have gone out.'

'It was nothing much. Nuna and Skip dealt with it. They had no intention of calling you. I only knew about it because I went over there to look for you when I got back. The patient's fine.'

'Excuse me, I'll go over there.'

'It's OK, Alanna.' He took her arm. 'The patient's OK.'

She pulled away, pushing past him. 'I must go.' Without bothering to get a coat, she ran through the covered walkway to the medical station, then hurried through the clinic to the ward area where the post-partum patient was being cared for by Nuna, in a separate room from John with the tracheostomy.

All was quiet and serene there as Alanna arrived, breathless. Nuna was sitting near the sleeping mother, at a table lit by a shaded lamp. Next to her was the baby, sleeping in a canvas cot slung from a metal frame.

'Hello, Nuna. Everything all right?' she whispered.

Nuna was stitching brightly coloured beads on to a piece of soft suede leather. As she smiled at Alanna, her smooth round face glowing in the lamplight, her black eyes almost disappeared from view above her plump cheeks. She wore a simple white overall, her hair pulled back in a bun.

'Everything fine,' she said quietly. 'I take her blood-pressure every half-hour, her pulse every few minutes. She don't wake up. There was a little bleed earlier on; we got it stopped quickly with uterine massage.'

'How much blood did she lose?'

'Maybe 250 ml. . .something like that. We had the IV going at the time, so OK. We kept it in. It's because she have seven kids, all born close together,' Nuna continued bluntly. 'Too many. The uterus not contract properly afterwards, so bleed.'

'Yes. I'll just have a look at her. . .and I want to do a haemoglobin test, then you call me if there's the slightest problem. How's the baby?' Alanna bent over the cot to see the tiny baby, bundled up in a yellow blanket.

'Baby fine,' Nuna said.

On her way out through the clinic later, having done the test and ascertained that the haemoglobin was within normal limits, and after checking up on their tracheostomy patient also, Alanna decided to put through a call to Bonnie Mae, who would probably still be awake.

'They stopped it pretty quickly, so Skip told me,' Bonnie explained. 'It was no big deal, Alanna.' She paused. 'Has Doc been putting the pressure on you?'

'Sort of. . . I certainly feel guilty about going out.'

'Don't. You need to get out, have some fun. I have Chuck to help me forget work. You see, Alanna, it's a luxury for us to have doctors available. Not so long ago there was no doctor here, so we're used to dealing with things on our own. There's no way I'd want to return to the bad old days, but there's no need for you to feel guilty either. OK?'

'Yes. Thanks, Bonnie. Goodnight.'

To her relief, Owen was in his room when she returned, so she quickly went to her own room to make preparations for sleep. It had certainly been a long day. Under the hot shower she mulled over all that had happened. Tomorrow, Saturday, they would take out John's tracheostomy tube, then in a day or two he could go home. Their post-partum patient and her baby would go home on Sunday if there were no more signs of bleeding, and if she didn't discharge herself before then. There was no routine work to be done over the weekend; they would all take turns caring for the two in-patients, then relax for the remainder of the time. Officially it was Owen's day off tomorrow.

The Northern Medical Development Corps had asked her and Owen to supply them with independent monthly reports of their cases, and suggestions about ways and means of improving medical services in the northern areas. Tomorrow she would begin her first report.

She was brushing her damp hair when a knock came

on her door. Quickly she put a robe on over her nightdress before opening it.

'Just wanted to check that everything's OK over there before I go to bed.' Owen wore a dark towelling robe. The lapels gaped to reveal a tanned chest liberally covered with dark hair. Alanna was aware that she made an automatic scrutiny of him, down to his bare legs and feet, unable to help herself. His hair, like her own, was damp from the shower, his face freshly shaven.

'Everything's all right,' she said. 'Nuna and Skip are there, as you know. I — er — I assume that we'll be taking out John's tube tomorrow?'

'Yes. . . I also wanted to apologise, yet again, for seeming to pressure you. It's a habit I got into in the past.' His soft drawl lent a caressing note to the apology. 'Not much to do with you really.'

'I do appreciate that you have some justification for being zealous about what goes on at the clinic. . .'

'Yes. . .' He sighed. 'But I'm always testing. I will get over it before too long, I promise. Goodnight.' The kiss that he gave her on the cheek was unexpected, as were the warm fingers on her neck as he held her briefly. Then he let his hand fall away from her. 'Sleep tight.' For a few seconds he stood looking at her, his gaze going over her involuntarily, from her coppery hair down to her slippered feet, as she had looked at him.

'Goodnight, Owen. Don't forget your own advice about inappropriate liaisons,' she whispered, and shut the door.

For some obscure reason she felt ashamed. . .perhaps because she could not hold out a hand to him silently and invite him into her bed. She wanted to do it, so much. . .knowing that he did too, perhaps in spite of his better judgement. Regretfully she acknowledged that she lacked the experience, the right level of sophistication, the courage to do it. So the moment had passed.

The wind sighed and gusted around the building as she lay awake, a sound that was now familiar, as though all the great spirits of nature had gathered there. The Inuit would perhaps explain it that way. Somewhere in the village a dog howled. Waiting for sleep to come, she thought about the patients she had seen over the last week, about Yodelling Joe, about Tim. . .and Owen Bentall.

CHAPTER EIGHT

THE days passed, then the weeks. Very slowly the snow melted in and around Chalmers Bay, leaving a landscape like crazy paving, where persistent patches of ice showed pale among the mud and gravel that was now revealed. Little rocky outcrops came into view where a short while ago the pristine snow had glittered in the sunlight. At last the temperature rose above freezing point, so that it stood at between three and four degrees in mid-June, with the air clear and sweet. There was a steady drip of melting ice from rooftops. There were no longer fresh falls of snow in the night. The days lengthened, then, following on from a period of strange twilight instead of darkness, there was light twenty-four hours a day.

In the village the numerous skidoos gave way to motorised three-wheeler, all-terrain bikes, which had enormous fat tyres to grip the unpaved roads and to cushion the rider. Teenagers and their younger brothers and sisters were out on them, speeding along the side-roads, laughing and calling to each other, basking in the heady promise of summer. In the weeks that she had been there, Alanna had learnt to drive both types of vehicle, as well as the medical station's pick-up truck. She took to walking out much more around Chalmers Bay, then out on to the tundra, taking care to carry the rifle and not stray too far from the buildings. Since the weather had started to warm up, Owen had arranged some trips for her out of Chalmers Bay by helicopter, or in a light Cessna plane. They would land for a short while in an accessible place, then walk.

On these walks the mystique of the North had gradually begun to take on a reality in the shape of living things. They saw migrating caribou, flocks of snow geese and other birds flying to their breeding grounds, polar bears in the distance and, once, a black bear, then a family of wolves. Underfoot, struggling up from patches of persistent, clinging ice, were springy clumps of low scrub. Owen told her the names of the plants—juniper, cranberry, crowberry, cloudberry. Purple saxifrage, not yet in flower, grew bravely between rocks covered with lichens of purple, orange, silver and gold. Alanna was entranced with it all, with the sights and sounds of this burgeoning life.

When they flew over the water of Coronation Gulf they saw white whales cavorting in the icy waters, and the mysterious narwhals, glimpsed briefly, breaking the surface of the water with their speckled bodies and long, whirled tusks. As she gazed, Owen mainly watched her, telling her only what she wanted to know, not trying to overwhelm her with his superior knowledge and experience. She respected him for that.

'Wednesday, the first of July,' Bonnie Mae announced in the clinic office at the end of the day's operating list, to anyone who cared to be reminded of the date, while they were all drinking coffee. For once they had no inpatients, the last one having recovered from the operation and departed. Skip was there taking a much needed rest before starting on the clearing-up and resterilisation of instruments. 'When are you planning to take your vacation, Skip?' Bonnie eyed the large wall calendar.

'Oh. . . August, I guess.'

'Maybe I'll go later this month,' Bonnie said, making tentative marks in pencil on the calendar. 'Maybe take two weeks to go to Edmonton. Chuck may take a week off then, even though it's the height of the season for him work-wise. Is that OK with you, Doc? Gives you enough time to get a replacement?'

'Sure. Let me know soon, when it's firm. The Medical Corps sends us someone from Edmonton,' Owen explained for Alanna's benefit. 'Usually someone who's been here before.'

'Usually we get Anne Lawson,' Bonnie Mae added. 'She's great! Been here several times. Tough as old boots, but really nice underneath.'

Alanna watched Owen smile at some secret thoughts of his own. Since the middle of May, the evening he had kissed her on the cheek, they had not been alone a great deal in the evenings as darkness had given way to constant daylight. There was no need for them to sit in the claustrophobic sitting-room if they didn't want to. Occasionally she found herself, perversely, longing to be really alone with him.

'Want to come on a couple of house calls with me, Alanna, before you quit for the day?' Bonnie asked lightly. There was something overly casual about her tone that made Alanna accept without questioning her.

'Yes, I'd like to.'

'Great! We can either walk or take the truck. There's Charlie Patychuk to see, then the baby that was born on Sunday. I'll be ready in about ten minutes.'

'Let's walk.' Alanna stood up, taking off the lab coat that covered her green scrub suit. 'We should be getting the X-ray report back soon from Edmonton, *re* Charlie's chest X-rays. It seems to be a long time coming.'

'I think you can probably reassure him,' Owen

interjected. 'I couldn't see anything on them that we didn't know already.'

'Yeah. . .' Bonnie said crisply. 'I don't suppose Charlie's holding his breath waiting. He'll just be getting on with life, and smoking while he's at it!'

'Did I detect an enigmatic note in your voice, Bonnie?' They were walking briskly away from the medical station along a newly revealed path that led round the back of some buildings.

'You sure did. I've been waiting for a chance to tell you all day. Chuck phoned me last night about those enquiries he's been making. There's some guy at the Moose Lake weather station, friend of his, who has an entry in his log that he says is definitely from our medical station, on the day that Dr Cooke would have made it. Right time, too.'

'Oh, Bonnie, are you sure?' Alanna stopped in excitement, oblivious to the patch of mud into which her boots were sinking.

'As sure as I can be. Chuck's coming to Chalmers for the weekend; he'll be here on Friday for the square dance at the church hall. He's bringing several photo-copies of the log entry. The guy at Moose Lake is a bit of a fanatic for accuracy, so he said, and keeps all records for years.'

'That's wonderful!' Impulsively Alanna hugged Bonnie. 'I can hardly believe it, after all this time. I've been writing to my brother; I think he's beginning to give up hope.'

Charlie Patychuk was sitting out of bed, ensconced in the small sitting-room of his daughter's house, whittling at a piece of bone with a knife. A lighted cigarette smouldered in an ashtray beside him as he worked.

'*Nani nunaqaqaqpit?*' he enquired, after Alanna had taken his blood-pressure and listened to his chest once again, noting a distinct improvement.

'He's asking you what place you come from,' Bonnie Mae informed her.

'From England.' Alanna smiled at the old man.

'Ah. . .' he said, nodding his head.

'He doesn't feel like speaking English today,' Bonnie explained quietly as they departed. 'Sometimes he likes to assert himself that way.'

From there they went on to see the mother and child, then back to the medical station.

'Goodnight, Bonnie,' Alanna said. 'When you speak to Chuck, tell him I'm enormously grateful for what he's done.'

'You'll see him at the weekend. Will you be going to the square dance at the church hall? Get Doc to escort you. They're great fun, and we don't get many of them.'

'I'd love to come.' She smiled at a mental vision of Owen Bentall galloping around the floor in an energetic square dance. 'With or without Dr Bentall.'

'Well, goodnight. See you tomorrow.'

That evening she and Owen worked on the disaster plan for the Northern Medical Development Corps. Owen's trips to the mines were helping all people concerned to put together a plan to deal with major emergencies in and around Chalmers Bay. Where mines were concerned, there was always the potential for terrible disaster. They worked well together on the task, sipping white wine as they bent over their notes and charts at the dining-table in the annexe. Putting it all together into a fail-safe working arrangement was a challenge. This was the first evening that they had really spent together, for a sustained period, for quite some time without the presence of at least one other person.

They were so at ease, working so well together, she thought, when their concerns centred on work matters. For the rest of the time, they both seemed too aware of a strong mutual attraction, of inappropriate liaisons, to be anything other than prickly.

'Let's call it a day, shall we? Perhaps we can begin to wind it all up over the weekend, then I can send off the first draft to the NMDC.' Owen stood up, stretching, looking very casual in jeans and a sweater. 'I'm bushed. How about some sandwiches and coffee, Dr Hargrove?' he said teasingly. 'Hmm?'

'That would be lovely.' She struggled to her feet clumsily. 'I'll make it.'

'No. . .no, you just relax.'

Alanna gave a sigh of contentment as she heard him whistling tunelessly in their tiny kitchen. It was strange that in spite of occasional pangs of homesickness there was no other place she would rather be at this moment, no other person she would rather be with.

'What are you thinking, pensive Dr Hargrove?' Owen was observing her through the hatch.

'Well. . .actually I was thinking how well we work together, which is ironical when I think of how mean you were to me on first meeting.' She pushed untidy tendrils of hair away from her face self-consciously.

'Yes, I quite agree. . .on both counts. I have apologised. Unless you want me to go down on bended knee.'

'As much as I would like to see that,' she laughed, 'it's not necessary right now.' Not for the first time, she wished that he were not so attractive. Even if he had a face like the back of a bus, as her mother would have said, his personality would have ensnared her. Yes. . .

her thoughts drifted. . .she would love him, no matter what. My God, don't say that, she admonished herself sharply, as though she had actually spoken. Don't even think it.

To cover her consternation, she stood up and turned on the radio. It was true, of course. In a kind of hopeless way, she adored him. Which was why she could not bear him too close, didn't want him to touch her, in case she gave herself away, made a fool of herself. After all, she had four months left in which she had to work with him. She knew that he was sexually attracted to her, probably nothing more. This was an interlude in her life that would soon be over; then they would each return to their very separate lives and she would never see Owen Bentall again. Never was a long time. . .

The radio station was playing a medley of old songs from musical shows. As the sound filled the room, the jocularity of it seemed forced and dated to her; it grated on her nerves. She reached to turn it off.

'Don't switch off, Alanna.' Owen had come into the room, carrying two plates of sandwiches. 'We could use a bit of noise. Come and have your sandwich.' Just then a song came forth from the radio with a renewed crescendo of sound. 'I like these old songs. . .a bit *passé*, but a refreshing change from some of the modern cynicism,' he added, moving over to turn up the volume.

The strains of the well-known song 'Shall We Dance?' blasted out. When Owen turned to her he mouthed the same question, taking her into his arms, holding her in the manner of an old-time waltz, and she went willingly. There wasn't much space in the sitting-room. As they danced around the table they moved closer together, until both his arms encircled her firmly.

Then a slow, sentimental song replaced the more energetic one, so that they moved languorously between the chairs and table, their bodies touching. Alanna closed her eyes, giving in to the sensations that his proximity aroused.

'Any minute now,' she said, 'we'll get a call to do an appendectomy.'

'Or to see an inebriated seaman with a fish-bone stuck in his throat,' he offered.

As they laughed together, she again had the feeling like the one at the weather station where they had landed on the way to Chalmers Bay. . .that their relationship was undergoing a change. What that change was she did not understand at the moment, when his presence was so immediate, his face so close to her own.

'Alanna, you have the most beautiful eyes. . .like the eyes of a fawn in dappled sunlight,' he said softly, his face uncharacteristically tender as he regarded her, unlike his usual assessing glance of hard intelligence. 'They give away your every mood and thought. . .did you know?'

'No. . . I didn't know I was that transparent.'

The slow smile that curved his mouth told her that the expression in her eyes did indeed give her away. She parted her lips involuntarily as his eyes focused on them, waiting for the kiss that was now inevitable. Will-power seemed to drain from her as they stood together in a close embrace, in the room that had witnessed many previous withdrawn and polite exchanges between them. When the music stopped, replaced by the announcer's voice, the kiss ended. Owen drew back, holding her at arm's length, the expression in his eyes warm, enigmatic. If he had asked her to share his bed then she would have agreed. He did not ask.

'Eat your sandwiches,' he said lightly. 'The coffee is coming right up.' He went back to the kitchen, while she sat down again and forced herself to eat.

'These sandwiches are delicious,' she called. 'Better hurry up; I might start on yours.'

They drank their coffee watching a rather out-of-date news programme on television. At least, Alanna pretended to watch, keeping her eyes either on the screen or on her coffee-mug, tensely aware of Owen a few feet away.

'Goodnight, Owen,' she said, standing up.

He looked up at her, his expression unreadable. 'Goodnight, honey,' he said.

The next two days were very busy, but fortunately with no in-patients. Now that the weather was warming up and the local residents were getting out more, the staff at the medical station had started a publicity campaign in Chalmers Bay to get them to come in for routine chest X-rays to guard against tuberculosis. There was always something for Alanna to do, so that she often found herself having to make an effort to take time off.

On the Friday she found time after the operating list to walk to the postal station to pick up their mail. There was a satisfying number of letters for her—from her mother and Tim in England, from her married sister in Australia, as well as from friends who very clearly thought she would be feeling terribly isolated. Impatient to read the letters, she took a walk to the waterfront area to find a quiet spot in which to read them before returning to the annexe, starting on her mother's letter.

Considerably later, Alanna let herself into the annexe, to hear the telephone shrilling in her room. When she answered it, Bonnie's voice, terse and hurried, came loud in her ear before she had a chance to say hello. 'Alanna? Doc's on his way over there to see you. Chuck was here a few minutes ago; he spilled the beans in front of Doc. . .about Dr Cooke and the Moose Lake weather station. . .about him being your brother and all. Gee, I'm sorry, Alanna; I didn't know he was going to open his big yap! I'd told him to keep quiet about it, but he assumed that Doc knew.' Her voice rose on a shrill note of apology.

'It's all right, Bonnie. Can't be helped. I had to tell him some time, didn't I? It might as well be now. How much does he know?'

'Everything.'

'Don't worry, I'll deal with it. Thanks for warning me.' As she put down the receiver she heard the outer door open and close.

With a sigh she took off her jacket and flung it on the bed, then went into the bathroom and locked the door, annoyed with herself because her heart was pounding. As she washed her hands and brushed her hair she reasoned with herself that it should not matter one way or the other that she was Tim's sister; it was a fact that had not affected her work adversely. Indeed, it had made her more careful and cautious. So, she might as well confront him.

He was waiting for her in the sitting-room, in one of the armchairs, and he rose to his feet as she entered. The expression on his face was closed, withdrawn.

'So you're Tim Cooke's sister. Why didn't you tell me?' he asked brusquely, standing squarely in front of her.

'What difference does it make?' Alanna decided that attack was the best form of defence. 'I had intended to tell you eventually. It was a question of choosing the right moment. The reason I didn't tell you initially was that Tim had told me you were not sympathetic to his situation, so I assumed that you would not have any sympathy with my cause either, to find out more information. . .to confirm certain things. You would have been more hostile to me than you were already,' she rushed on. 'Besides, the NMDC might not have hired me —— '

'I did have empathy with his situation,' he interrupted her. 'It wasn't my place to be sympathetic to him; I was supposed to be impartial and I tried to be. A baby was dead. If anything, my sympathy was with it.'

'Yes, I know,' she said, her voice sounding clipped and curt, even to her own ears, because of mounting apprehension. 'Tim did all he could; it wasn't his fault; he was overruled by Dr Debray. There's proof now that he put out emergency calls to aircraft on his own initiative.'

'So you came here to Chalmers Bay to find that out? And all the time I was thinking that you had come here to do your bit for the North, for the native people here, that you might possibly be persuaded to come here again. Isn't that a bit like being here under false pretences?'

'No. . . I did come here because I wanted to do something for Chalmers Bay. . .to help with the disaster plan. . .'

'Would you have come if you weren't Tim Cooke's sister? Would you have even entertained the idea?' he persisted, looking at her broodingly.

'I. . . I don't know.' She moved away from him, not meeting his eyes. 'Yes, I think I would have. Even before Tim came here, I knew about jobs in Chalmers Bay.'

'I doubt that you would have come. Why can't your brother fight his own battles?'

'He did all he could while he was here; he had to leave. Later he practically had a breakdown because of all the false accusations, the cover-ups, the blame put on him.'

'What did you hope to achieve?' He had come to stand close again, glaring at her.

'Perhaps to get the inquiry reopened, to clear his name, set the record straight.' The quaver in her voice betrayed the tears that were gathering in her eyes.

'Why didn't you tell me earlier?' he repeated.

'What for? Tim told me you were arrogant. . . ruthless. He felt that you could have helped more at the time. After encountering your attitude on the flight up here, I was inclined to agree with him.' The atmosphere in the room was decidedly unpleasant.

'Actually,' he said, 'I admired Dr Cooke a great deal . . .the way he dealt with the situation. As I believe I said earlier, he was a good doctor. . .'

Alanna blinked rapidly, not looking at him. 'You said other, less complimentary things. . .'

'As it turned out,' he went on, 'the inquiry was of the opinion that Dr Debray had tried to save his own skin. As I recall, Tim Cooke was more or less exonerated.'

'"More or less,"' she reiterated bitterly. 'That's not good enough for my brother. No one seemed to believe that he put out those emergency calls. . .that he had wanted to operate immediately. He wants proof, then a written exoneration from the appropriate authorities, even if the inquiry is not exactly reopened.'

'That would involve a certain amount of work, time and money.'

'Yes. Tim's reputation is worth it.'

'Naturally you would take your brother's side.' He fixed her with a cold stare. 'You're asking quite a lot.'

'I don't think so,' she said, clenching her fists. 'Especially now with the Moose Lake evidence.'

With hands thrust into the pockets of his white lab coat, he began to pace restlessly in the confined space, so that she tensed when he came near her. 'You expect me to do something about it?' he said.

'Not necessarily you. . . I don't expect anything of you. There are four months left for me to decide what to do, then to do it.'

'Four months? You mean you're going to stick it out to the bitter end?'

'Yes. . .' She looked at him in surprise. 'Of course.'

'There's no "of course" about it! Now that you've got what you want, I imagine that you'll ship out of here at the earliest opportunity, certainly before the winter sets in. It's the same old story.' There was a jeering note in his voice.

'I shall do no such thing; I'll honour my contract,' she said angrily.

'The NMDC is trying to build up a team of people who would want to come back here from time to time,' he said, ignoring her protest. 'You could consider that you're getting a training here, not just a job. You are not likely to come back.'

'Don't make sweeping assumptions about me. I'm not Gloria.' The words came out with difficulty. Her lips, her whole face, felt stiff with the effort of keeping her expression under control. 'And I'm not answerable to you.'

They were both breathing heavily. At no time since their arrival at Chalmers Bay had Alanna seen him so pale and tense — she assumed with anger — the pallor emphasising the straight black eyebrows that were drawn together in a frown above his cold eyes. 'You're over-reacting,' she said.

'Oh, yeah? I've spent a lot of time and effort orientating you to this place. . .the whole bloody system. And to think I admired you for coming here! I guess I still do. . .for coming for such an esoteric reason. . . I've seen a lot of people ship out of here on an hour's notice. They get the next plane out when they realise they can't hack it. You haven't much incentive to hang on now.'

'Who said I can't hack it? I've said I intend to honour my contract.' She met his derisive gaze unflinchingly.

'Oh, yeah?' he said again, his North American accent very pronounced.

'Sometimes I hate you,' she said quietly. There must be some way to get through his screen of certainty that she was going to let him down, was going to renege.

'Hah!' The sound was harsh. 'Only sometimes?' Then, as they stood facing each other like animals squaring off for a fight, the expression in his eyes slowly changed, until she could read there very clearly that he was recalling the evening two days ago when she had returned his kiss eagerly. Any minute now he might remind her that hate was akin to love. What would he care if he knew that she was really in a turmoil over him? All he really cared about was getting the medical station staffed. He didn't change.

Unable to bear the tension any longer, she headed for the kitchen, muttering, 'Excuse me,' as she went, hoping he would take the hint that the discussion was at an end. There was nothing more to say. In the kitchen she clattered about, making tea. Her throat felt restricted with the need to cry. The memory of Tim as he had been on his return to England was fresh in her mind. . .anxious and depressed. . .unable to work. . . unable to concentrate on anything. . .

Mercifully, Owen Bentall did not follow her,

although she knew he had not left the sitting-room, was waiting for her to come out. A few tears dribbled from her eyes and she wiped them away with a tea-towel. For the first time the lack of privacy seemed like a burden. Slowly she went through the motions of making tea, prolonging it as much as possible, and stood drinking it with her back to the open serving-hatch.

'Aren't you going to offer me tea?' he called from the next room.

'You come and get it yourself!' Instantly she realised her mistake. He would see that she was about to cry; she would be trapped there. Hastily, clumsily, she scrubbed at her face with the tea-towel. Keeping her face averted, she bent over the sink to wash the few plates that were there while he helped himself to tea. For God's sake leave! her whole body screamed at him silently.

'By the way,' he said, his voice neutral, 'why have you a different name from Dr Cooke? Are you perhaps married? Divorced. . .maybe?'

'No. . .' She looked at him then, her guard down. 'Neither.'

The expression on his face altered to something approaching concern, albeit guarded, as he saw her anguished eyes. Too late she turned away, feeling again the tears gathering.

'Nice cup of tea, Alanna,' he said conversationally.

'Oh, shut up!' She turned away from him, holding the bunched-up tea-towel against her mouth. How could she ever regain any dignity with him now?

'Look. . . Alanna, I will try to help, to see what I can do,' he said quietly, just behind her.

'You don't have to,' she blurted. 'I didn't ask for your help.'

'None the less, I want to help.'

'Since when?' she asked, as viciously as her sadness would allow. 'Since twenty seconds ago?'

'No. . . Being bitchy doesn't suit you.'

'What does suit me? Being humble in your presence?' She kept her back to him, hearing him sigh.

'Don't forget, Alanna, that I was around for the inquiry. I do understand.'

'Perhaps you do. . .some of it. What you can't know is how devastated we all were. . .my family. Everything has been a struggle; we can't afford to lose anything. . . least of all a reputation on which a livelihood depends.' The bitterness in her voice silenced him for a while as she strove to regain her composure. When he put a hand warmly on her shoulder she flinched.

'Let's talk about this some time over the weekend, when we can maybe look at it more dispassionately. I accept that I have no right to make assumptions,' he said gently, reasonably. Chameleon-like he seemed to have changed again.

'Don't touch.' She shrugged off his hand. He sighed again.

'Can't we be friends?' he said softly. 'We were friends.'

She was in danger of crying again, not necessarily for Tim. 'Go away. . .please.'

'No!'

Just when Alanna was beginning to think that they might be standing in the kitchen for the rest of the evening, with her face to the wall while he waited for her to unbend a little, Bonnie Mae entered the sitting-room, having come in noisily through the double doors from the covered walkway. This was the first time she had entered the annexe without being invited.

'Hi there, you two.' She caught sight of them in the kitchen and took in everything at a glance. 'My conscience was bothering me; I thought I'd better come over to see what was going on, seeing as I was responsible. You've been crying, Alanna. . . My, my. You ought not to have done that, Doc. I can't stand by and see you bully her.'

'He thinks I'm going to take this opportunity to leave, Bonnie, now that I've got the information. I'm not, of course.'

'Silly man! Now, we're all going out for the evening, to the church hall. There's going to be a barbecue with the dance, so we can eat there. We're going to forget about this place for a few hours. I've arranged for Skip to stay here for the evening. . .he doesn't much care for square dancing. So I reckon you've got no choice. As for you, Doc, she needs your protection.'

The church hall, when they entered later, was packed with people standing and sitting around the sides, leaving a space in the middle for dancing. It was noisy and warm, the lights dim, with a white haze of cigarette smoke hanging like a fog beneath the low ceiling. It mingled with smoke from the smoke pots that had been set up outside around the area of the door to keep off the thousands of mosquitoes that rose up from the burgeoning tundra in the evening, from their breeding grounds in the moist vegetation.

Two fiddlers and an accordion player stood on a low dais by the bar, while a 'caller', a wizened elderly man, belted out the traditional dancing instructions into a microphone. 'Swing your partner, round you go, do it again, then a doh-ce-doh.'

Owen took Alanna's arm as they moved through the crowd to an ante-room at the back where they could leave their coats. Alanna was glad of the raucous noise. Then Chuck, who was enormous and bearded, 'a real big guy' as Greg Farley had described him, whirled her away into the centre of the square dance, expertly putting her through the moves that she had never made before, leaving Bonnie temporarily to cope with her colleague. There was a certain satisfaction in feeling her cotton muslin skirt swishing against her legs as Chuck swung her round. . .of leaving Owen Bentall in the capable clutches of Bonnie Mae.

CHAPTER NINE

FOR the next few nights she scarcely slept, welcoming any work that came her way with an almost masochistic relief. Since the confrontation over her brother the annexe seemed to have become too small for the two of them, Owen's presence too pervasive, although neither of them had referred to it again. Over the weekend they had finished the first draft of the disaster plan.

During the Tuesday night they were both called for a Caesarian section, Owen being the one on call. When he telephoned her room for the medical station she had actually been asleep. 'Can you come over and do a cross-match before we get started?' he asked. 'I've taken the blood for testing; it's in the lab. It's Lynne Nanchook. . .she's gone into premature labour.'

'Oh, no! Will she be all right?'

'There's no foetal distress at the moment, so we'll keep our fingers crossed. The baby's heart-rate is good and strong. The problem will be later. . .dealing with a premature baby round the clock. Lynne stayed at home until the membranes had ruptured.' Owen's voice was curt, showing his obvious annoyance. 'That's one way of getting out of going to the city.'

'She couldn't help going into labour, though.' Alanna felt an urge to defend the Inuit woman, while knowing that Owen was at least partially right. 'Anyway, I'm on my way over.'

'I'm going to do an epidural anaesthetic so that we can both scrub. Skip's coming in as well,' he added.

By the time she reached the operating-room, having

first set up the blood samples and the donor samples for the cross-match, everything was organised by the two nurses, with Skip already scrubbed and Bonnie Mae helping Owen with the epidural anaesthetic. When the blood for possible transfusion was finally ready they were waiting for her, so that all she had to do was to scrub and put on a sterile gown and gloves.

Lynne Nanchook remained awake but sedated, the lower part of her body anaesthetised, an oxygen mask clamped to her face to ensure that her baby would be well-supplied.

'Hello,' Alanna bent down to smile at their patient reassuringly, seeing a predominant expression of relief in the young woman's eyes. 'Everything's going to be fine.' Lynne's eyes smiled back at her above the black rubber mask that covered her nose and mouth, obviously pleased to see her as well as the other familiar figures.

'She took care to miss the five o'clock plane to Edmonton,' Owen chipped in, making their patient look a little sheepish.

Alanna moved to take up her position on the opposite side of the operating table from Owen, where everything was ready for them to make a start. Then Skip passed the scalpel silently.

As Owen made the horizontal incision in the patient's lower abdomen, a bikini incision, so that she would not have a noticeable scar later, he told Alanna in a low voice about the recent obstetrical history. Lynne had been in labour for some time at home without telling anyone until the membranes had ruptured. Now there were signs that the labour was not progressing as it should, and the baby was still in the breech position. Once the membranes were ruptured it was better to get the baby out within a certain length of time because of possible infection.

It was necessary for them to move quickly. Owen worked deftly and expertly, very calm. When the lower segment of the uterus was exposed he made an incision into it, while Alanna swabbed and clamped. As they cut through to the cavity of the uterus there was a sudden rush of amniotic fluid, which she was prepared for with the suction nozzle ready. The baby's bottom was immediately visible, overlaid with a piece of the pale, opalescent amniotic sac. They extricated the presenting part of the baby through the incision, then the rest of the body was born with another rush of fluid. Gently they eased out the baby's head.

This was always an emotional moment, when a new human being arrived in the world, a pinkish-grey colour, still attached to its mother by the thick, twisted umbilical cord. Alanna clamped and cut the cord while Owen held the baby with its head downwards to allow the mucus and fluid to drain out of its nose and mouth. Already it was making a few grunting and whimpering noises, making tentative waving motions with its tiny slippery arms, preparatory to the first positive yell of life during which it would draw air into its lungs for the first time. The whole procedure had taken only a few minutes.

'It's a girl!' Bonnie Mae exclaimed, standing by with a fresh suction apparatus. 'You've got a lovely girl! Looks a good weight, too.'

Lynne turned her head to look as Owen placed the baby on the sterile drapes in the infant-resuscitation cart, with that peculiar expression of relief and joy on her face that was characteristic of new mothers when they beheld the seeming miracle of their own baby in the flesh. As she smiled, a few tears eased from the corners of her eyes and rolled slowly down her face. Alanna looked away, back to the task in hand, feeling tears prick her own eyes. The baby was going to be all right. Unlike the baby that Tim had delivered in similar circumstances. . .

The nurse immediately suctioned out mucus from the baby's airway. In a few seconds the room was filled with the mewling, lusty cry of the new-born, a sound that was the most positive in the world and one that never failed to bring a surge of emotion to Alanna, no matter how many times she had heard it or seen the process of birth. For a premature baby, Lynne's daughter was a good size, waving her arms vigorously as she yelled.

'Perhaps her dates were wrong, after all,' Alanna suggested to Owen quietly, her eyes drawn to the beautiful baby.

'Maybe,' he agreed. 'Keep suctioning, please, Dr Hargrove.' She looked up quickly to see Owen eyeing her with an expression that she could only interpret as tender amusement. 'Your turn will come.'

She could have hit him. 'Sorry,' she said.

'And no, you can't hit me with that retractor,' he added lightly. 'We need to keep it sterile.'

'You're quite a mind-reader, Dr Bentall,' she said, gripping the large retractor so that her knuckles shone white through the thin rubber of her gloves. 'A good thing you don't know all of it.' She applied the suction nozzle vigorously with her free hand. He laughed softly, obviously letting his imagination run riot.

'Everything's just fine, Mrs Nanchook.' Owen peered over the sterile screen that they had erected to separate the head of the table from the operating field. 'You just relax there. We'll get you off this table in no time.'

There was a collective air of relief in the room. The worst was over. The placenta was lifted out of the uterus through the incision, as the uterus began to contract to stop the bleeding. They prepared to sew up.

'Number one Chromic catgut, Skip, please.'

'OK, Dr Bentall. Ready for the sponge count.'

When they were eventually back in the annexe, to sleep for what was left of the night, Owen made tea for them without asking if she wanted any. Exhausted, Alanna sat in a chair in the sitting-room, her shoes off, not bothering to put on the light. She closed her eyes, which felt dry and gritty once again from lack of sleep, her throat parched.

'Thanks,' she murmured as he thrust the mug of hot tea into her hands and took the chair near her. The blessed liquid was very hot and sweet. For a while they drank in silence, sitting in the dim light that emanated from the kitchen. 'One good thing to be said for total exhaustion,' she mused eventually, 'is that it drives everything else from your mind.' She and Owen Bentall were at ease with each other once more, or as much at ease as they would ever be.

'Mm. . . It's a short operating list tomorrow,' he offered. 'We needn't get up at the crack of dawn. Bonnie will have arranged for some relief for herself . . .and someone to be with the baby constantly. I'm sure that baby will be fine. More tea, Alanna?'

'Please. It's nice, isn't it, that we haven't got the energy for verbal battles?'

He chuckled. 'Sure. . .' Then when he came back with the tea he remained standing in front of her. 'By the way, Bonnie told me today that she definitely wants to take two weeks off, starting on the nineteenth. I was thinking that we ought to get the hell out of here for a few days before she goes, otherwise we'll be into August before we can take any time off. We could take off this weekend for four days. Bonnie could hold the fort. . .we could be back here very quickly if need be. What do you say?'

Because he stood in front of her with his back to the light she could not see the expression on his face, while she was conscious that hers must show a quickening interest tempered by an apprehension that such a trip might precipitate some sort of showdown between them for which she did not feel quite ready.

'Actually, there's nothing I'd like more at the moment than to get away from here for a few days. Where. . .where would we go? And how?'

He sat down again. 'We'd take a Cessna. . .maybe follow the Coppermine river down to the treeline; it's not far by air. There's a small lake in an area that I know pretty well, and a place to land a plane. . .or maybe we'll land on the lake. We could take a couple of tents and a rubber dinghy to paddle around the lake, do some fishing. If we had more time we could take a canoe down river. As it is, a dinghy will do fine. . . easier to get on one of those small planes.'

'It sounds wonderful!'

'Do you mean that?' he asked quietly. 'Am I forgiven for any boorishness that you've endured?'

'Yes. . . I've been less than honest with you about my brother. . .by omission.'

'Mm. . .that's settled, then. How about if we leave on Saturday? Assuming that it's OK with Bonnie. Lynne Nanchook should be fine by then.'

'Sounds all right to me,' she agreed. A quickening of excitement revived her spirits, although a question nagged at her. 'Owen. . .did you take Gloria there? To this lake you're talking about?'

'No. I've always been alone when I've been there on other occasions. Gloria isn't the outdoor type. She loves cities.' His voice was neutral.

'Then why did she come up here?'

He hesitated. 'Would you believe me if I said it was because she thought I would be good husband material . . .that she thought by coming up here to live with me she could clinch the marriage deal? Does that sound insufferable, arrogant?'

'Well. . .' She paused, trying to choose her words carefully. 'It does. . .but I don't disbelieve it.'

'That sounds hellishly cynical, I know. I was pretty naïve when I met Gloria. Up here things sorted themselves out quickly. There isn't much room for subterfuge in a place like this. Anyway, why do you ask?'

'I wouldn't. . .sort of. . .want to follow in her footsteps. . .in any way.'

'Neither would I want you to. Rest assured that you are nothing like Gloria, in any way. OK?'

'Yes. Thank you for suggesting the trip. I can't wait to see you blowing up a rubber dinghy!'

'You're very welcome. You're a brave girl for accepting,' he countered, smiling. 'And those dinghies are self-inflating. . .sorry to disappoint you.'

'Oh, well. I'm sure there will be plenty of other sights to keep me entertained.' Alanna stood up, feeling a renewed lightness of heart. So far he had made no direct reference to her emotional outburst of the other night. . .unless calling her a girl was a hint. 'Goodnight, Owen. I must get some sleep or I'm going to collapse. And I'm not a "girl."'

'Sorry. . .just an expression. I had noticed that you're very much a woman, in more ways than one. Goodnight, Alanna.'

For the first time in quite a while she slept like the proverbial log.

* * *

It was a Cessna with pontoons that flew them out of Chalmers Bay harbour on Saturday morning, heading a little west and then south. Soon they could see the Coppermine river, cutting through the landscape beneath them, which they were going to follow to get to the lake where they were to camp. The tiny plane was stacked with their belongings and supplies for the three nights and four days that they would be there. Buck, the Indian pilot, was to come back to pick them up on the Tuesday at twelve noon precisely.

The landscape, not far below them, was a motley mixture of greys, greens and browns, the river the colour of chrome. Small lakes of fantastic shapes were dotted like blobs of protoplasm in the barren land as they moved further south. Chalmers Bay might not have existed.

Very conscious of Owen beside her, Alanna nevertheless relaxed and gave in to the inevitable physical contact between them. Every so often they exchanged smiles, both delighting in the Arctic scenery and, in her case, in his company. She stopped short of speculating about what he really thought of her. Surely Tim had been wrong about him. . .

Far in the distance ahead of them she could see trees. From maps that they had studied she was aware that the treeline curved upwards towards the north the further west one went, as the temperature warmed nearer to the Pacific Ocean, then dipped again sharply eastwards where there were no warming sea currents to temper the extreme cold.

The lake where they were to camp, Mirror Lake, came into view not long after they spotted the first trees. Owen pointed it out to her, not bothering to talk above the engine noise. True to its name, it lay as still and shiny as a looking-glass, reflecting the sun and the

stunted spruce trees that grew around its edges. Here
and there were small bays where a light plane with
wheels could possibly land. With their pontoons they
would be landing on the water. The Cessna lost height,
then circled the lake for a landing approach. Alanna
leaned back in her seat, keeping her eyes on the back of
Buck's head, on his thick black hair that he had pulled
back in a ponytail with an elastic band. His casualness
belied his obvious expertise.

Owen reached for a pair of fisherman's waders that
he had stashed under the seat and pulled them on,
giving Alanna a conspiratorial wink as she scrutinised
his efforts with interest. She had vaguely assumed that
they would paddle ashore in the dinghy. The landing
was smooth, in the centre of the lake. Plumes of water
reared up from the pontoons on either side of them.
Buck pulled back the throttle to slow them down, then
moved the plane as far as he dared towards the shallow
water of a small stony bay before cutting the engine.

'Thanks a million, Buck,' Owen said, then turned to
Alanna. 'I'm going to carry you ashore, then we'll get
the dinghy inflated to land the rest of our gear. It's
pretty shallow here. You have to jump down on to the
pontoon first.'

'OK,' she said, using the local and universal lingo,
and feeling almost sick with excitement. The plane
shifted a little when they were both down on the
pontoon, then Owen eased himself into the water, the
level of which came up to his hips, several inches below
the top of the heavy waders.

'Crouch down,' he instructed, 'then put your arms
around my neck and lean forward.' When she had done
that, he put one arm around her waist and the other
under her knees and swung her against him, holding her

above the water. Slowly and carefully he waded ashore, the water becoming shallower with each step.

Buck waved as he took off, having called, 'See ya Tuesday.' They stood with their bundles of supplies and the dinghy on the shore, to watch while the plane circled the lake once then headed back towards Chalmers Bay, the sound like a buzzing bee becoming more and more distant.

When it was finally gone, Owen turned to her and put a finger to his lips. 'Shh! Listen!' At first there was only silence as they stood in the sunlight that was surprisingly hot. Then as her ears became attuned to their surroundings she heard a gentle lapping of the lake water against the shore, as though protesting its disturbance by man. Then she heard the movement of wind through the stunted Arctic willow out on the tundra just beyond the few spruce trees behind them. There was the dry rustle of spruce branches, then from somewhere among them a bird chirped. As the moments ticked by in the strange isolation, as they heard the small stirrings of nature, the full realisation came to Alanna that she was totally dependent on Owen. . .and he on her.

'When you've been here for a few days,' he said, 'it's so quiet you can hear the insects moving.'

'Yes, I can imagine. It's wonderful,' she said. 'Absolutely wonderful!'

Then the insects found them.

'Aagh. . . I'm being bitten!' She slapped at a blackfly that had landed on her cheek. 'Where are those bee-keeper's hats, Owen? Quick!' While he rummaged in a knapsack, she swatted the mosquitoes that were coming at them in droves.

'Zip up your jacket and tuck the legs of your jeans in your socks,' Owen instructed, grinning up at her. 'You look as though you've got a bad case of St Vitus's dance.'

'It's all right for you,' she chided him, 'you've probably got some sort of immunity to these things.'

'No such luck.' He pulled out two khaki-coloured bee-keeper's net hats and handed her one. 'Wait until you encounter the no-see-ums. They have a way of getting inside any net, then we have to barricade ourselves inside the tents.'

'"No-see-ums"! You must be joking!'

'I'm not. They're tiny dots, smaller than a pin head, and they pack a ferocious bite.'

With the net over her head, things were decidedly better. 'How come you glossed lightly over the insect question when you suggested this trip?' she teased, watching him peel off the waders. 'You certainly didn't mention those no-see-ums, so I'm wondering what else you forgot to tell me.'

'Oh. . .there may be the odd grizzly or brown bear. Telling you in advance would spoil my fun of having you rush to my tent in the middle of the night for protection.' His lean face, usually serious, was alight with enjoyment, not entirely at her expense.

'Oh, yeah!' She borrowed one of his favourite expressions again. 'I'm not sure that "protection" is the right word.'

'You have to suffer a little before you can enjoy the Arctic, Alanna. At least now that it's light all the time the bears aren't likely to creep up on us. Come on, let's get the tents up. We might as well camp right here in this bay. I'll rig up a tarp between two trees as a makeshift bathroom to give us a bit of privacy.' He began to drag their gear back from the water-line.

'What about all these insects? How can we do anything?'

'There are certain times when they're less prevalent. Out in the middle of the lake there won't be any either. If you could collect some driftwood and anything that will burn, get a fire going, I'll put up the tents. The smoke will keep off the bugs. You can consider this all part of your medical training, under the category "how to survive in the bush". OK?'

'OK. . .sure,' she said, with exaggerated sarcasm, grinning back at him. Then, feeling like a space walker in the net hat that came down to her shoulders to cover her head and neck, she began to look for wood and dried grass and leaves. They could not cut any wood from the precious trees.

'Don't wander too far away,' Owen called.

'Grizzlies, and all that?'

'Yeah.' When he smiled at her again her heart turned over. It was both good and disturbing to see him out of a work context, enthusiastic in a different way, endearingly boyish as he sorted out the components of their tents, his black hair curling untidily over his forehead. Yet very much a man. A very attractive man.

'Aren't you going to put on your net?'

'Sure.' Obligingly he donned the headgear. 'Have you got insect repellent on you for your hands?'

'Yes. . .thanks.' Abruptly she turned away, continuing her search for something to burn, conscious of being supremely happy. Even though it would be a strange four days, fraught with complex undercurrents, she was determined to enjoy each new experience as it came, to ignore a niggling worry that she should not be enjoying the company of this man when her brother's problems were not yet resolved. At least they would be in separate tents.

The smell of spruce came pungently to her nostrils as she moved among the trees. The only sound was the persistent high-pitched buzz of mosquitoes as they vainly tried to penetrate the net. The thin belt of trees soon gave way to tundra, now lush and green. She gazed at it, looking far, far into the distance. . .

Time moved quickly when there were no modern conveniences, when every simple, familiar activity became a long-winded chore. Yet they were chores that produced a sense of relaxation — coaxing a fire to keep burning with the maximum amount of smoke, filling pots of water from the lake to boil on a propane stove, stuffing chinks in the tent flaps with clothing to keep out insects.

When evening came, scarcely distinguishable from morning in the twenty-four-hour daylight, apart from the position of the sun, they had finished a supper of tinned soup, meat, and vegetables heated on the propane stove. Smoke from the fire was effectively keeping most of the insects away so that they could risk removing their headgear. Earlier they had explored a section of their side of the lake. The tents were up, two small one-man tents, with their entrance flaps facing each other.

They sat on large stones, drinking smoky tea, gazing out over the still surface of the looking-glass lake. 'Homesick?' Owen regarded her perceptively.

'A little. I try not to think about it too much. . .about how far away I am from anyone who really knows me, or cares. . .'

Sitting opposite her, leaning forward, Owen fixed her with that particular intent expression that he wore when he was trying to make a diagnosis on a difficult case. 'Is there. . .or has there ever been. . .anyone special. . . back home? I know I've asked you that before, indirectly; you never gave a very satisfactory answer.'

Out here she could not get up and go into the next room to escape his scrutiny. A feeling of waiting, of being suspended, held her in the knowledge that they were moving towards something. Anyway, she did not really want to escape, not any more.

'There was someone once. . .special. . .an older colleague. He was separated from his wife. . .or so he said. After I got involved with him I found out that he was seeing rather more of his wife than the term "separated" implied. . .so that ended.' The lightness of her tone was intended to disguise the old hurt that still lingered. Although she did not look at him, the loaded silence told her that he was not deceived.

'Hmm. . .so that accounts for your prickly attitude, would you say?' When she did not answer, he went on. 'You're wrong, you know, if you think no one here cares about you.'

'You, for instance, basically dislike me for being the wrong colleague, if nothing else.' She dared to meet him head-on. 'Bonnie Mae and Skip are great. . .they can't invest too much in me emotionally, knowing I'll soon be gone. Sometimes one feels very much alone. Not now, of course. This kind of aloneness, once in a while, is good for the soul.'

'I don't dislike you, basically or otherwise,' he said.

There was not going to be any escape for her. Soon, if she was as transparent as he had said she was, he would know that she loved him, and her vulnerability would be complete. All her life she seemed to have been striving for a certain independence. She felt it crumbling at the edges.

Owen poured more tea into their tin mugs from the billy-can in which two teabags floated. A few birds, sandpipers, totally unafraid, hopped over to peck at a chunk of bread that they had left on a plate. Absently Alanna watched them.

'I think we should talk. . .if you don't mind my taking advantage of you as a captive listener,' he said. 'On that day we saw the polar bear. . .afterwards. . . I already had some sort of proprietorial feeling for you . . .when I'd only set eyes on you four or five days before. It was ridiculous to feel so posssessive. Maybe that will give you an indication of how desperate I was for some female company. That was when I decided I had to pull back, otherwise come on too heavy.'

'Inappropriate liaisons?' she suggested quietly.

'Yeah. . .' The expression was self-deprecating, as he looked out unseeingly over the lake. 'It wasn't dislike . . .then or earlier. . .' His deep voice trailed off. All was still and quiet, bathed in muted orange light, as though listening and waiting, as she was.

'I'd just spent two and a half months of the winter here, on and off,' he continued. 'You sure go stir crazy then, if you're not careful. Then I had two weeks off . . .it wasn't enough. Then you come along, all fresh, young, beautiful, enthusiastic. . .'

'You don't have to give an account of yourself, Owen, I do understand.' She thought she understood that he was not particularly interested in her, Alanna Hargrove. He needed a woman and she happened to be there. Not that he would take any woman, of course, a voice mocked inside her head; she had to be of a certain appearance and accomplishment. Like the beautiful Gloria, whose photograph Bonnie had shown her one day. Until he got tired of her. That had taken about three weeks. Not suitable for the North. Unless there was love and friendship on both sides, how long would it take before boredom set in? How long would it take with her?

'How can you understand?' Owen continued to talk, as though to make up for the many silences between them. 'The winters are not like this. It's dark all the time. . .cold beyond description. A lot of the time you dare not leave the medical station. That's why I didn't want you here. Men play cards, play chess, watch movies interminably, drink beer. . .'

'And men and women make love, or "sleep together,"' she said pertly, breaking into his monologue. 'Or did you and Gloria call it "having sex"? That's the North American expression, I believe, isn't it? Especially when there's no love involved. A sort of business arrangement for the duration of your stay, with no strings attached? Hmm?'

Jumping up, she quickly gathered together the plates, cutlery and pots that they had used. 'This is summer now, Owen. What's supposed to happen now? Or are you about to show me?' She turned away from him, keeping her face averted. 'I understand what you're telling me: whatever happens, not to get too involved, not to expect too much. "Playing it cool", as you would say.'

'Alanna!'

She walked away, carrying the stuff to be washed down to the water's edge, ignoring his tense expostulation, taking her time over the task. They would become lovers, she knew that. Her longing for him was overwhelming. This beautiful, quiet place, where human life was frail, beckoned them towards a fusion of their separate entities, where to be separate was to be even more vulnerable than the loss of independence and control that threatened her so much.

When the pots were washed and stacked in a box, she took off her hiking boots and socks and waded into the icy water so that it came just above her ankles.

'Cold?' Owen's voice sounded just behind her.

'Freezing!' When she looked over her shoulder, forcing a smile, he was barefooted, coming towards her. 'Does it ever warm up?' She steeled herself against his longed-for touch, unsure.

'Not much.' He stood behind her, putting his arms round her, pulling her back against him as she stared over the wide lake to the distant shore where the clusters of spruce trees stood like hazy, dark sentinels. 'Don't be angry with me; I don't want your disapproval.'

'I'm not angry.'

'What, then?' He bent his head to put his cheek against her hair. When she did not answer, he added, 'Are you frightened of me? Of being here alone with me? If you are, you don't have to be.'

'No. . .not really of you. More of myself. . .of how I'll feel if I get involved with you.'

He might have said, Go with the flow, or something equally superficial, but he did not. Instead, he held her steadily, brushed his lips against her hair where it met the sensitive skin of her temple.

'What will you do when you leave the Arctic?' she asked.

'This time I'll resume my vacation, go somewhere hot. Then I guess I'll go back to Vancouver Island to work with my father. It would be good to come back up here for two or three months a year, preferably in the summer, to help keep up a certain continuity.' Although he did not ask her what she would be doing, the unspoken question seemed to be hanging heavily in the air between them.

'Were you happy as a child. . .close to your parents?' she asked.

'Not particularly close; they were always working.

That came first with them. That's not something I would want for my own children. I don't think I'm obsessed with career moves the way they were. As for being happy. . . I guess I was as happy as the average kid. And you?'

'Same for me. . .and for Tim. . .although we were pushed very hard to be independent because there was nothing much for us to fall back on.'

'You certainly achieved that. . .and you're frightened of losing it.'

'Yes.' For a few more moments she enjoyed his closeness, then reluctantly shifted. 'My feet are turning to blocks of ice; we'd better move.'

'We could paddle out there in the dinghy, now if you like, right to the centre. It's a great view; you can see all round the edge of the lake. No bugs either.'

'Yes, I'd like that.' She turned round to him enthusiastically, to see his eyes soft with a tenderness for her that was startling. 'Owen, I. . .'

Not sure what she had been about to say, only knowing that she wanted to be very close to him, her words died away and he responded to her, knowing exactly what she wanted from him. The sharp flare of desire in his expression as his eyes searched her face complemented her own. When they kissed it was with the desperation of two people who had been long alone, their other brief contacts only a dress rehearsal for this, which was to be the real thing. All that remained was the question of when. Soon, very soon, when they were both ready, regardless of the consequences.

'Come on.' He held her hand as they went ashore. 'We'd better put on warm socks before we each have a cardiac arrest from the chill.'

'I'm going to risk changing into shorts, mosquitoes be damned.'

In her tent she dried her cold feet, then looked through her rucksack for shorts and clean socks before stripping off her jeans and sweatshirt. The tent, of dark green canvas, with a darker green fly-sheet extending beyond its sides all round, was pleasantly warm and cosy, the interior bathed in a dim green light.

'Alanna.' Owen was outside the entrance flap to her tent. 'There's something I want to tell you before we go out on the lake. Could I come in for a moment? I hadn't planned to tell you yet. I changed my mind.'

'Oh. . .wait a second.' She scrambled to put on the voluminous sweatshirt again. Kneeling on the sleeping-bag that was spread out over the floor of the tent, she opened the flaps to let him in. 'Come in quickly; don't let any bugs in.'

Once in, he stretched out full-length on her sleeping-bag, lying on his side, while she knelt beside him feeling a little exposed with her bare legs and feet. Yet having lived with him for weeks she found him dear and familiar, as well as disturbing. 'What's so urgent? Is there a group of grizzlies out there on the tundra, or something?'

'No. . .nothing like that. To get to the point. . .there was a letter from Dan McCormick over a week ago. Remember Dan? Apparently his leg is more or less OK now. He offered to relieve me up here. That is, he would come up here and I would go. After all, it was really his tour of duty.'

In the few seconds following this totally unexpected statement Alanna stared at him, feeling her lips part in surprise and shock. 'But I. . . I thought. . . I assumed that you would stay. To the end of October, that is. Until I go.'

'It seems he's quite willing to resume his duties any time, and stay until the end of October.' Owen was

watching her. He could see clearly the alarm that had
flared in her face. Strange, she had scarcely given
another thought to Dan McCormick since she had
arrived in Chalmers Bay.

'What did you tell him?' she whispered.

'I haven't replied yet,' he said evenly. 'I'm considering his offer, and I wanted your opinion first.'

Alanna shifted her position so that she was partly
turned away from him. You can't go. . .you can't, she
wanted to shout. 'You mean I have a say?' she asked
quietly, not looking at him. 'Do you want to go?'

'Sure you have a say. I wouldn't go if you would not
feel at ease now with a change. It would be nice in some
ways to resume my normal life. . .since I hadn't
planned to be here now.'

'That doesn't really answer the question.'

With a sigh he lay down flat on his back, with his
hands behind his head. 'In other ways I don't particularly want to go. We have more work to do on the
disaster plan. . . Do you care one way or the other? Do
you want me to go?'

'No. . .no. Of course not. I wouldn't want to start
again with someone else. We work well together. . .
and I've got used to living with you.' The idea of getting
used to someone else in the annexe was daunting.

'Is that all?'

'Yes. . .no. I'd miss you. . . I've got used to you,' she
repeated. When he did not reply, she risked a look at
him and found that he was watching her with a tautness
that belied the casual stance of hands behind his head,
legs crossed at the ankles. Don't you care? She wanted
to scream the question at him.

'Is that all?' he persisted.

'No. . .'

Owen took a deep breath and let it out on a sigh,

reducing the tension. An admission of sorts had been made, verbally on her part. Apropos of nothing in particular, he said, 'I'm scared of committing myself in case it turns out wrong. You're scared of losing your independence, even though you love me.'

Fear and surprise startled her into turning fully towards him, to dropping any guard that she had left. The fear now was that he would slip away from her. 'Very perceptive of you,' she said in a low voice. 'You're right, of course. I'm truly sorry, Owen. . . I know you didn't want to. . .to get entangled in that way. We come from two different worlds. In a few weeks we'll be going our separate ways, if not before. In the meantime, I do want to continue to work with you. . .if you'll do me the favour of staying on. That's my position, but. . .any decision you make must be independent of what I want. . .'

'What is there to be sorry for?' he said softly. 'Things happen. . .predicted or otherwise. Even so, they don't always turn out exactly as one predicts.' He sat up, so that his face was close to hers, both shadowed by the soothing reflected green light. They could hear the soft scamper of birds alighting on the tent.

'You thought I would be the one to take off. But I won't be. . .' There was a note of desperation in her voice. This, as the locals said, was a whole new ball game. 'I'm going to be here until the end of October, no matter what, and I would prefer to be with you, although I'm sure that Dan would be a super person to work with.'

'You're quite something. . .quite a woman!'

'No. I only take on things I know I can cope with. So what will you tell Dan?' The poignancy of her situation was almost more than she could bear. She wanted to rant and rave.

'In a few days I'll telephone him.' When he put out a hand to touch her face, to smooth his thumb delicately over her lips, she did not retreat. Instead, her eyes sought his in an admission of love as she swayed towards him. 'I can't see myself getting out and leaving you to him,' he said.

They looked at each other in the tense quiet of their wilderness surroundings. A slow smile transformed the introspective stillness of his features. 'So you only take on things you can cope with! Can you cope with me? Because I as sure as hell want you.'

He brushed his lips briefly against hers, a movement that sent a wave of heat and longing through her body. There was no point in pretending to misunderstand him, in pretending that he had made an admission of love to match her own. Neither was there any point in deluding herself that she did not want him physically as he wanted her, that a mere delicate touch from him did not leave her without resistance.

'Yes. . .' she whispered. Very deliberately she crossed her arms in front of her chest and lifted the thick sweatshirt over her head in a slow, graceful movement, letting it fall unheeded beside her as she shook out her tangled hair, feeling her heart thudding in anticipation as the cool air shocked her bare skin.

Owen did not move. His eyes locked with hers, his pupils widening, darkening with desire as she reached to unclasp her bra and to shrug out of it, impatiently freeing her breasts to his gaze. When, at last, he reached out to take both her breasts in his hands, then to bring his mouth to touch the cleft between them, she moaned like a small, trapped animal.

'Undress me. . . Alanna.' Taking both her hands, he placed them on his chest. 'Don't be frightened. . .take your time. . .darling. . .'

As her hands fumbled with the buttons of his shirt he kissed her neck, her shoulders, then his mouth found hers and he thrust his tongue through her unresisting lips, deep into her mouth. Convulsively she pushed the shirt from him, then held his head closer to her, tangling her fingers in his thick hair, letting him know that she wanted him to kiss her like that. . .in a way that no man had kissed her before. . .she wanted everything to be different with him. . . Capturing her hands again, he moved them down to his belt, keeping his hands warmly over hers as he helped her to undress him. He gave a primitive sound of pleasure, deep in his throat, as she touched his skin.

Unashamedly naked, looking like a bronzed god to her heightened awareness, he eased her down beside him as, shyly, she looked at his aroused body. They were both trembling and their breathing sounded loud in the small, sun-warmed tent, as he finished undressing her, letting his hands linger. A sensual smile of triumph blazed in his face as he looked down at her. . . There was lust in that smile when his gaze moved slowly, possessively over her body, yet when his eyes met hers as he leaned forward to touch her mouth with his there was a warmth and affection as well, a strange vulnerability. . .

'Owen. . . I must know. . .' She breathed the words urgently. 'Were you indulging in emotional blackmail . . .by waiting until now to tell me about Dan?'

'You could say that,' he admitted, speaking against her mouth, teasing her lips with his. 'Was my timing good?' As he spoke he touched her confidently, delicately, from her sensitised breasts down over the curve of her hip to the soft inner skin of her thighs.

'Perfect. . .' she whispered, arching her body upwards to meet his caressing fingers.

'To misquote Hamlet,' he murmured huskily, moving over her, ''Tis nice to lie between maids' legs.'

Then there was no more talking as she welcomed him to her, welcomed his crushing weight on her body as he enveloped her in his strong arms, as his mouth captured hers and held her silent. . .as she gave herself up to his frenzied, mindless passion. . .feeling herself losing all sense of time, of place. . .aware only of his thrusting maleness and her own, all-consuming pleasure.

It was very much later when they sat side by side in the dinghy, moving out slowly, lazily towards the centre of the lake, through the silver-coloured water that was perfectly smooth, its surface shot through from the west by a blood-red line of light from the orange ball in the sky that was the sun. Owen had shown her how to hold the wooden paddle, how to move it through the water at right angles to the side of the dinghy. Sometimes they paddled, sometimes they just drifted along, delighting in the gentle rocking motion of their craft. When Alanna looked over the side she could see her face perfectly reflected against the towering dome of the sky. Somehow she expected herself to be changed, in keeping with her inner transformation, to see the love that suffused her blazing there. Instead, her face looked back at her serenely.

Dressed in corduroy trousers and a casual wind-breaker over a checked shirt, Owen looked ruggedly handsome, although still the sophisticated professional man. Yet somehow there was something different about him, a softness, an intimation of a letting go of an iron will. It was there in his face as they smiled at each other.

They did not say much as they moved out languidly, in emotional accord, to the centre of the lake, from

where the far shore could be seen mistily, dark and
mysterious. Alanna's body felt bruised and totally
sensitised to the presence of the man beside her, as
though he was now an irrevocable part of her. Never
before had she felt like this about any other man and
she knew intuitively that she never would again. Never
before had she felt so womanly, so feminine, so aware
of a man as the opposite of herself. . .that mysterious
other that made her complete.

They rested the paddles in the bottom of the dinghy,
then simultaneously they moved into each other's arms,
hungry to make contact, his mouth searching for hers.

'It's midnight. . . I bet you didn't realise,' he said
when he let her go. Then he turned her gently to face
the orange light. 'And that's the midnight sun.'

CHAPTER TEN

ON THE Tuesday evening Alanna found herself walking through Chalmers Bay to make a house call on Charlie Patychuk, their pneumonia patient, while Owen had gone to check on Lynne Nanchook and her baby, who had been discharged home.

Frequently she had felt sure there must be something more sinister in Charlie's lungs than simple pneumonia or some chronic fibrosis, because of the duration of his illness. Now the radiology report was back from the university hospital in Edmonton, saying that he had some chronic emphysema and signs of old tuberculosis but no cancer, so she had decided to go over in person to see him.

It was a beautiful evening, the sun lighting the colourful, low houses in a balmy glow. People sat out on their porches, or ambled lazily along the lanes. They waved to her and called out as she passed, 'Hi, Doctor,' or, 'Hi, Doc,' or, 'Doing OK?' They had accepted her, she knew that, and hugged the knowledge to her with satisfaction. All her hard work and effort seemed justified, especially as several children walked along beside her, asking her where she had been going in the Cessna the week before. Not much escaped notice in Chalmers Bay. They would be asking her when she and Owen were getting married next — the persistent thought came to her and she tried to push it aside with an unaccustomed irritability.

Charlie Patychuk was also sitting out on his porch, with a bottle of beer on the floor beside him. Inevitably he had a cigarette in his hand. She mounted the steps quickly to escape the increasingly searching questions of the accompanying children. 'Bye now,' she said to them. 'I'll see you later.' Reluctantly they withdrew, with many backward glances.

Deciding to ignore Charlie's smoking, she sat down beside him on a bench. 'Hello, Mr Patychuk. How are you?'

'Great, just great,' he said, his weathered face displaying its full gamut of creases as he smiled, evidently in a mood to speak English today. 'And how are you?'

They talked for some time after she had conveyed the good news from the X-ray report. Charlie became animated when she told him of her trip to Mirror Lake, from where she had returned only a few hours before. Although he was not at ease with English, his vocabulary limited, he struggled to converse with her. It was apparent that he knew the land around there intimately, as well as every nuance and mood of the lake itself.

As they lapsed into silence once more the old man seemed to tap into her mood of mingled elation and pensive longing that her time with Owen had engendered, with an uncanny empathy that seemed prophetic in some way.

'Good to see the sun all day, all night,' he commented. 'It remind us to take life while we can.' He made a motion of catching and pulling something invisible towards him. 'Some of my people believe. . . with the midnight sun the Great Spirit come. . .out there where all silent. . .to give you what you ask.'

'Do you believe?'

'Yes.' He looked at her shrewdly. 'But it is you. . . must be ready to take.' When she got up to go, he briefly clasped her hand. '*Matna*, *tiguaq*. Goodbye. I will see you again soon.'

That simple man, in tune with nature in the old way, had somehow sensed her underlying despair. Tears gathered in her eyes as she walked quickly along the back lanes towards the medical station, skirting the edge of the tundra to avoid the usual entourage of children. For some reason she seemed to be crying very easily these days. He had thanked her in his own language, had called her *tiguaq*, 'adopted child'.

The time at Mirror Lake had been an ecstatic, miraculous time for her, during which she and Owen had scarcely noted the passing hours that had all blended together into a continuous long day of enjoyment. They had explored the lake, from the shore and on the water, had walked over the springy vegetation of the tundra, eating wild berries and looking at the flowers.

Now it was all over, never to be forgotten. A sadness like a sense of mourning enveloped her as she walked. She was the one now who was feeling possessive; she did not want to share Owen with anyone or anything — not his work, his colleagues, nor any woman he had ever known. She was jealous of the absent Gloria.

When they had made love she had whispered time and again that she loved him, while he had not committed himself in words. With his hands and body, with his urgency, he had shown how much he needed her physically. . .and how much he was able to give. Now that she knew, she would be tied to him emotionally forever.

Work returned to the usual pattern of routine and sudden, often dramatic emergencies. Bonnie Mae duly went on holiday, to be replaced by Anne Lawson from

Edmonton who knew the place well, a quiet, efficient nurse with a rare, earthy sense of humour. Alanna liked her instantly and the feeling was mutual.

'We were wrong, it seems,' Alanna challenged Owen late one evening as they lay together in her bed, the curtains drawn over the window. 'Being like this hasn't affected our working relationship, has it? In fact, it's never been better.'

'Mm. . .agreed. It might not have been earlier. We were just ready. . .like I'm ready now.' As he spoke, his eyes smiling at her, he ran a hand over her shoulder and her bare breast, causing her to murmur with pleasure and press her face against the side of his neck where the muscles were taut as he leaned over her, still shy that he should read the surrender that showed there.

'Don't hide from me. . .'

'Do you think Bonnie knows about us?' she mumbled against him, kissing his salty skin.

'Sure. Not much gets past Bonnie. It's what she wanted. She must have been very aware of the angst between us. One could almost hear her thinking, For God's sake, get on with it! She'll be relieved.'

'Mm. . . Have you contacted Dan yet?'

'No. . . I'm keeping my options open.' He kissed her, teasing. 'Since it's Saturday tomorrow, shall we stay in bed all day, only to emerge if duty calls?' he whispered against her ear, his breath making her pelvic nerves tingle sharply with sexual longing. 'I want to be like this with you all the time.'

'Yes. . .please.'

'Touch me, then, sweetheart. Show me how much you want me.' He was laughing, delighting in her acquiescence.

* * *

Alanna was aware that she was living from day to day, not daring to think about what would happen at the end of October. When Owen was away visiting the mines she pined for him with an intensity she had not thought possible, then later contrived to go with him whenever it could be arranged. If this was a hint of things to come, the possibility of separation terrified her. Sometimes she felt she was running in a race, being forced to run faster as she became more tired. Thus she tried harder to keep thoughts of the future at bay.

Things came to a head between them much more quickly than she would ever have anticipated. Bonnie Mae returned from holiday on a Monday, the third of August, and Owen departed two days later for the Black Lake mine, with the promise that he would call in at the Moose Lake weather station *en route* to speak to the radio operator who had picked up the message from Tim Cooke. Already Owen had made moves to ensure that the inquiry would be reopened in the near future. With his departure, it was as though the race of Alanna's life speeded up even more.

The day after he had left, fire broke out during the night at a house in Chalmers Bay, spreading to two more houses before it could be put out.

'It's serious, Alanna.' The telephone had woken her from sleep after a rare early bedtime, with a direct call from outside to the annexe. Greg Farley's terse voice described the problem to her. 'There are people with burns. As far as I can tell,' he said, 'not too bad, except one — that's Tommy Patychuk. The fire started at his place. He would have been OK, but he went back in to rescue a dog and the roof collapsed on him. He's in pretty bad shape with the burns.'

'Oh, no. . .not Tom. . .not Tom!' Her cry was anguished. A sharp remembrance came to her of the thin, shy native boy as she had first seen him at the clinic, proudly showing her his dog. 'The dog. . .?' she asked urgently. 'Is the dog OK?'

'Yeah. . .yeah,' the RCMP officer answered. 'It wasn't in the house anyway; it was outside all the time. That's the pathetic part of it. . . See you at the clinic.'

When Alanna ran to the window and pulled aside the curtains she could see huge plumes of black smoke drifting upwards. The wooden houses of the village would burn very rapidly.

Decisions formed in her head of their own accord. First she put through a call to Bonnie in her quarters. 'I'll need lots of warm, sterile saline, sterile towels, morphine, intravenous lines and a central venous line, as well as the cut-down set,' she instructed. 'I'll call Owen back here, then get on to the airport. Better call in Skip.'

It took her only a few seconds to put on clothing. Instinct told her to bring a jacket, her handbag and a toothbrush. Over in the medical station she put through a call to the Black Lake mine. When Owen's voice eventually came on the line, indistinctly, she told him the news, ending with, 'Get back here, Owen. Stat!'

Without waiting for a definite response, she cut him off and contacted the airstrip. 'This is Dr Hargrove,' she said. 'I need a flight to Edmonton, urgently. Please hold or contact all suitable planes. And I want you to keep a careful record of this call and your progress in finding a flight. I don't want any screw-ups.'

When Tommy Patychuk arrived on the back of a pick-up truck it was all Alanna could do to stifle a cry of horror and anguish as they removed the blankets that covered him.

'It probably looks worse than it is,' Bonnie Mae whispered, gripping her arm tightly for a few seconds in commiseration before they both set to work on him. He was black from head to foot, his burned clothing stuck to his puny body, while the skin of his lower arms and hands hung loosely, peeling off like gloves, to reveal redness underneath.

'We won't try to remove all the clothing, Bonnie. We'll wrap him in the sterile towels soaked in saline. I'll need some petroleum-jelly gauze too. He must be kept warm. I want two IVs going, if we can find veins. . . I'll probably have to do a cut-down. We'll put one in the leg. Good. . .you've got the morphine drawn up.' She spoke levelly, yet unable to keep emotion out of her voice.

Miraculously, Tom's face, although black with soot, had been spared. It still looked smooth and boyish beneath the singed hair. He was shivering and moaning with pain, fully conscious. The greatest danger with burns was shock, Alanna reminded herself, brought on by loss of body fluid and severe pain, bringing with it acute kidney failure as the blood-pressure dropped.

Side by side, she and Bonnie, with Skip helping, worked to save him. Those patients with lesser burns would be given pain-killers and first aid by Skip and would then have to wait for further medical attention.

'Don't let me die, Dr Hargrove.' Tommy looked at her, able to move only his eyes because of pain.

'No, Tom, I wouldn't do that.' She spoke with more certainty than she felt as she drew on a pair of sterile gloves. 'We're going to give you something to take away the pain. You'll be all right, my darling.'

'OK,' he whispered, total trust mingled with the expression of pain as he seemed to relax.

In that moment, with tears blurring her vision, she knew that she was in love with the North and its people, as she was in love with Owen Bentall; that she was

needed here, that she would be back. . .with him or
without him. When she was next out under the midnight
sun she would ask the Great Spirit what to do.

She was away in Edmonton for five days, having been
lucky enough to get a fast, direct flight out of Chalmers
Bay with Tommy and an aunt who had volunteered to
accompany them and remain in the city until the boy's
condition was stable. They left before Owen had
returned. Once in the city, with Tom installed at the big
teaching hospital, she decided to stay until she could be
sure that he would pull through, and to keep the aunt
company. The native woman was lost and frightened in
the teeming city.

From there she called Owen to let him know what
was happening. For once she felt that she had really
taken charge and come out intact, a big boost to her
professional confidence, even though that confidence
was tempered by the sober reality of Tom's condition.
Owen, in turn, told her that he had got the ball well and
truly rolling as far as the inquiry involving Tim was
concerned.

Her return flight landed in Chalmers Bay during the
evening of her fifth absent day. There was a feeling of
having come home as she walked away from the plane
towards the terminal building with the other passengers, mainly because the man she loved was here, and
she was half expecting Owen to be waiting there for
her. If he had been, she would have run into his arms.
In fact, no one was there to meet her. She looked
around her carefully in the building as gradually the
others dispersed.

'Dr Hargrove?' A man approached her from an
office.

'Yes. . .'

'There's a message for you, ma'am, from Dr Bentall at the medical station. He said to wait here until he can get to meet you. . .he won't be long. They had an emergency operation to do, he said.'

'Oh, I see. . . All right, I'll wait. Thank you.'

'There's coffee, ma'am, in the office, if you'd like some. You can wait there.'

'Thank you.'

As Alanna helped herself to coffee she kept a watch from the window for Owen in the pick-up truck. She felt absolutely drained, was still wearing the crumpled scrub suit under her jacket that she had worn on the night of the fire. A large wall mirror showed her pale face, tired, devoid of all make-up, her eyes large and shadowed, the whole surrounded by a mass of untidy hair. Turning away, she waited for Owen to come, not caring what she looked like, seeing only in her mind's eye the blackened, frightened face of Tommy Patychuk.

At last she could see the truck coming through the village towards her, bumping and weaving around the pot-holes in the unpaved road, and the sense of impatience and breathless waiting increased within her. When Owen came striding purposefully into the terminal she was ready for him in the main lounge. Silently they went into each other's arms, as though the separation had been for years. Through the blur of her own fatigue she was shocked to see how pale and haggard he looked. She closed her eyes for a few seconds, relaxing against the reassuring hardness of his body.

'Darling. . .sweetheart. . . I missed you like hell,' he said tersely, holding her so tightly that she could not breathe. 'Are you OK?'

'Yes. . .' She felt her lips trembling. 'I've missed you too. . .so much.'

He kissed her then, as though he wanted to devour her, to take her into himself, oblivious of the curious, amused stares of the few workmen who wandered through the building.

'Come on, let's get out of here.' He took her hand, looking around them. 'No luggage? I guess you didn't have time to pack a bag?'

'No. . .'

With an arm around her, half carrying her, he shepherded her out quickly to the waiting truck that had been carelessly parked at the entrance, then bundled her into the passenger seat and slammed the door decisively. Then she let the tears fall unashamedly, tears for Tommy Patychuk, only vaguely noting that Owen had swung the truck in a wide curve away from the village towards the open tundra, taking a narrow dirt track that went towards a rocky outcrop where the bay curved inwards to meet the scrub of the barrens.

Very soon the road, such as it was, came to an end and the truck bounced and reared over the low vegetation as Owen spun the wheel this way and that with a scarcely controlled savagery, his foot stamping on the accelerator to get as much power as possible out of the battered vehicle. Behind the shelter of the stark, looming rocks he brought it to a standstill.

'Get out,' he commanded her. 'Get some fresh air.' When they both stood at the side of the truck, away from the village, he reached for her. 'Come here. It's all right, honey, it's all right.' Owen held her convulsively against him. 'Tom's going to be OK now, thanks to you. You did a fantastic job on him. I'm proud of you. The whole village knows.'

'He's so young,' she said heartbrokenly. 'Only a kid really. . .a dear, sweet boy; he went back into the house to rescue a dog. Now there's nothing left of it. . . the whole place burned to the ground.'

'It's OK. The community will take care of them,' he said gently. 'It always does.'

'Such a sweet boy,' she repeated, unable to get the vivid impression of the injured boy from the forefront of her mind. 'His skin was hanging off in strips. . .his hands. There was nothing much I could do about it. Oh, my God, Owen. . . I felt so useless.'

'You did plenty. All that anyone could have done at that stage. You saved his life. He's going to need skin grafts now, if there's any good skin left to graft. If not, they'll try a donor, or artificial skin.'

'My professional weakness is that I can't stand seeing children injured or in pain. The thing is, you can explain to an adult. . .'

'I know. . . I know.' Owen leaned back against the truck and took her into his arms so that she was sheltered from the wind. 'He's going to be all right. . . just keep on thinking about that. We can both take another trip down to see him. . .soon. The family will take turns going down too, so that he'll never be alone.'

They stood together for a long time, listening to the sighing, soothing wind. Alanna rested a damp cheek against Owen's voluminous jacket as she looked out over the tundra. At their feet she could see the purple saxifrage in bloom, could feel the scratchy touch of the Arctic willow against her legs through the thin cotton of the scrub suit.

Presently she raised her face for him to kiss her, closing her eyes against the power of the sun, feeling the tension and sadness gradually lessen as his mouth moved on hers, coaxing a warm longing that she knew would soon blot out everything else, as though he was willing her by the power of his personality to forget. He unzipped his jacket, cocooning them together in its enveloping warmth, then purposefully insinuated his hands up under her suit to cover her breasts as her arms clung to his shoulders.

'Just warming my hands. . .in the best way I know,' he said, with mock-apology.

'Mm. . .they certainly need it. What conditions do I have to meet in order to come here again with you?' she whispered, many moments later.

'I'll tell you in a few minutes,' he murmured. 'First of all I want to do this. . .' Moving his hands down over her hips, inside her clothing, he touched the soft skin of her thighs. 'And this. . .'

When she moved even closer to him in response, revelling in his familiar caresses, he smiled his satisfaction. Yet he was not relaxed; there was a wild tension in him. 'I want to be quite, quite sure of you. . . Can't take any chances,' he said. As he caressed her intimately she whimpered, everything else gone from her mind in the ecstasy that swamped her. . .

'Owen. . . Owen. . .someone might see us. . .' The words were forced from her eventually in a sudden awareness of her lack of modesty as he kicked the lower half of her scrub suit away from their feet.

'Not a chance.' His voice was breathless against her ear. 'They all know about us in the village. . .they know we're out here. They'll give us a wide berth. . .at least for the next three hours or so.'

'You mean they'll all. . .know?'

'Sure! Every man jack of them!'

'Oh. . .' A heat that seemed to start in her chest quickly spread over her whole body. 'Oh. . .'

'No kidding!' he said, sliding other impeding articles of clothing down her unresisting body, moving them aside with his foot impatiently.

'Oh. . .' she whispered again as he touched her, reciprocating by moving her hands under his shirt to find his warm skin.

'Live with me, Alanna. . .permanently,' he said urgently. 'Marry me. . .whatever you want. . . That's my condition. Stay with me always. Please. . .don't say no. I'll do anything to have you. . . We could live in England, if that's what you want. . .or on Vancouver Island. . .or anywhere, come to that. We could return here every so often, on a contract basis. We'd make a great team. . .at work and out of work. . .it's not just the physical thing with us. I thought it would never happen to me. . .'

Laughing and crying at the same time, Alanna looked up into his face, which showed many emotions, a vulnerability mingled with the sexual desire and the determination to get a positive response from her. Definitely not arrogant now. 'I've known that for a long time,' she said calmly, tenderly. 'Darling, you know I love you. . . Yes, I will marry you. How could you doubt that? You didn't have to. . .'

'You mean I can stop?'

'Oh, no. . .no. . .please. Don't denigrate the "physical thing". . .'

With a great shout of glee and triumph he picked her up by the waist and swung her round and round, throwing back his head, laughing, all the tension gone from him.

'Owen, my clothes! Someone might see us. . .' In spite of her protest, her laughter joined with his, a wild sound, mingling with the summer wind from the ocean. 'Besides, it's cold. . .'

'You mean your lack of clothes! In that case, my darling. . .' laughing, he swung her up in his arms, through the open door to the cab of the truck '. . .we'll get under cover. . . Move over!'

When she slid along the wide seat he climbed up to join her. Her eyes widened as he began to unbutton the shirt that he had on under the jacket, then the buckle of his belt, his intent becoming clear. With his mesmerising gaze holding hers, he talked. 'We could get married at the Anglican church,' he said, purposefully undoing buttons. 'The villagers would love it. . .we could invite all of them. . .they could party for several days. The sooner the better, mm?'

'Yes. . .' She nodded, her love for him shining in her eyes. With the mention of the word 'love', it came home to her that he had not said he loved her. Those three words were not easy to say. . .

'Come here. . .' he commanded her huskily. Before she could move he had lifted her over on top of him so that her thighs straddled his bare hips and the coarse hair of his chest teased her exposed breasts as she lay against him. 'Mm. . .that's wonderful. . .sweetheart. . .' His head was flung back against the seat, his eyes glazed and unseeing, his lips parted. 'We'll come up here in the summer. . .when we're married. . .make love out on the tundra, among the flowers. . .' he murmured to her.

'Yes. . .please. . . Love me.'

Slowly he lifted his head up to look at her, focusing his eyes on her face. He lifted her hips above him as though she were weightless, so that he could enter her body, slowly, warmly. Mindlessly she reached for him, fitting herself against him as they became one, caressing his face, his hair, murmuring words of love. Behind her back he buttoned his wide jacket over both of them so that she was covered snugly, tight against him. 'You're wonderful. . .wonderful.' His voice was slurred as he seemed to let go of the iron will that seldom allowed him to relax completely, as he lost himself in the delight of her body. 'I could stay like this forever with you. . . forever. . .'

'Like this, and in every other way. I'm so glad I found you. . .' Alanna lay weakly against him, letting go. . . The whole population of the village could have come to stand around them and she would not have moved. Wave after wave of absolute pleasure moved through her body, sensitised as she was to his answering joy. For better or for worse she would take him. There could be nothing better.

'Yes. . .' he said, moving almost imperceptibly against her, holding her hips possessively against his. 'Forever. . . I love you. . . I adore you. . .everything about you.'

A flock of snow-geese flew low over where they sat, the soughing of their wings mingling with the human promises of love, as they all moved, in actuality and in spirit, towards the midnight sun. Alanna knew then that the Great Spirit had come to her, had touched her and answered her indirectly, fleetingly, as was her way. It was the way of the North, and she was *tiguaq*.

Full of Eastern Passion...

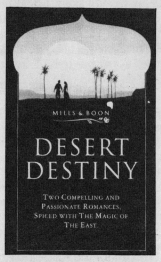

Savour the romance of the East this summer with
our two full-length compelling Romances,
wrapped together in one exciting volume.

AVAILABLE FROM 29 JULY 1994   PRICED £3.99

MILLS & BOON

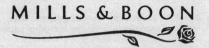

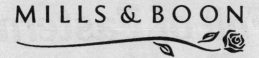

LOVE ON CALL
4 FREE BOOKS AND 2 FREE GIFTS
F R O M   M I L L S   &   B O O N

Capture all the drama and emotion of a hectic medical world when you accept 4 Love on Call romances PLUS a cuddly teddy bear and a mystery gift - absolutely FREE and without obligation. And, if you choose, go on to enjoy 4 exciting Love on Call romances every month for only £1.80 each! Be sure to return the coupon below today to: Mills & Boon Reader Service, FREEPOST, PO Box 236, Croydon, Surrey CR9 9EL.

-------- **NO STAMP REQUIRED** --------

YES! Please rush me 4 FREE Love on Call books and 2 FREE gifts! Please also reserve me a Reader Service subscription, which means I can look forward to receiving 4 brand new Love on Call books for only £7.20 every month, postage and packing FREE. If I choose not to subscribe, I shall write to you within 10 days and still keep my FREE books and gifts. I may cancel or suspend my subscription at any time. I am over 18 years. Please write in BLOCK CAPITALS.

Ms/Mrs/Miss/Mr _____ **EP63D**

Address _____

_____

Postcode _____ Signature _____